"Why do I want to kiss you?"
Burke asked huskily.

"I don't know," Cara murmured. "Maybe because I want to kiss you too."

His already simmering blood began to boil. He had never known such instantaneous need. It wound through his body, coiling around his chest, restricting his breathing so that he had trouble speaking again.

Carefully he slid his hand down her side, past her waist, around her hips. He pulled her against him. He wanted to feel her. He wanted her to feel him. He heard her gasp at the touch, then, with much less care, he crushed his mouth down on hers.

He was like no man she had ever kissed, Cara thought. Her instinct told her that he could be dangerous, her senses told her that his sexuality had an almost violent tinge to it. And even though she'd never faced anything like it before, she wasn't afraid. She wanted the experience of Burke Delaney. For this moment, she wanted to know everything he had to give her. . . .

WHAT ARE *LOVESWEPT* ROMANCES?

They are stories of true romance and touching emotion. We believe those two very important ingredients are constants in our highly sensual and very believable stories in the *LOVESWEPT* line. Our goal is to give you, the reader, stories of consistently high quality that may sometimes make you laugh, sometimes make you cry, but are always fresh and creative and contain many delightful surprises within their pages.

Most romance fans read an enormous number of books. Those they truly love, they keep. Others may be traded with friends and soon forgotten. We hope that each *LOVESWEPT* romance will be a treasure—a "keeper." We will always try to publish

LOVE STORIES YOU'LL NEVER FORGET
BY AUTHORS YOU'LL ALWAYS REMEMBER

The Editors

LOVESWEPT® • 169

Fayrene Preston
The Shamrock Trinity:
Burke, The Kingpin

BANTAM BOOKS
TORONTO • NEW YORK • LONDON • SYDNEY • AUCKLAND

THE SHAMROCK TRINITY: BURKE, THE KINGPIN
A Bantam Book / November 1986

LOVESWEPT and the wave device are registered
trademarks of Bantam Books, Inc. Registered in U.S. Patent
and Trademark Office and elsewhere.

Cover painting by Joe DeVito.

ISBN 0-553-21788-7

Published simultaneously in the United States and Canada

Bantam Books are published by Bantam Books, Inc. Its
trademark, consisting of the words "Bantam Books" and
the portrayal of a rooster, is Registered in U.S. Patent and
Trademark Office and in other countries. Marca Registrada.
Bantam Books, Inc., 666 Fifth Avenue, New York, New
York 10103.

PRINTED IN THE UNITED STATES OF AMERICA

O   0 9 8 7 6 5 4 3 2 1

This is dedicated to
Kay Hooper and Iris Johansen.
Ladies, it was truly a pleasure.

Preface

It was said that the Delaneys were descended from Irish kings and were still kissing cousins to half of Europe's royalty. Being more than an ocean away, Europe's royalty could scarcely confirm this.

Luckily for the Delaneys.

Old Shamus Delaney was wont to speak reminiscently of various cattle reivers, cutthroats, and smugglers in his family, but only when good Irish whiskey could pry such truths out of him. Sober, he held to it tooth and nail that the Delaneys were an aristocratic family—and woe to any man who dared dispute him.

They were a handsome family: tall and strong of body, quick and keen of mind. Nearly all of them had dark hair, but their eyes varied from Kelly-green to sky-blue, and it seemed at least one person of every generation boasted black eyes that could flash with Delaney temper or smile with Delaney charm.

None could deny that charm. And none could

deny that the Delaneys carved their empire with their own hands and wits. Royalty they may not have been, but if Arizona had been a country, the Delaneys would have been kings.

Whatever his bloodlines, Shamus Delaney sired strong sons, who in turn passed along the traits suitable to building an empire. Land was held in the teeth of opposition, and more was acquired until the empire spread over five states. Various businesses were tried; some abandoned and some maintained. Whenever there was a call to battle, the Delaney men took up arms and went to war.

Many never came home.

In the first generations, an Apache maiden caught a roving Delaney eye, and so the blood of another proud race enriched Delaney stock. Sometime before the turn of this century a Delaney daughter fell in love with a Spanish don who really could claim a royal heritage. She was widowed young, but her daughter married a Delaney cousin, so there was royal blood of a sort to boast of.

They were a canny lot, and clan loyalty was strong enough to weather the occasional dissensions that could tear other great families apart. The tides in their fortune rose and fell, but the Delaney luck never entirely deserted them. They built a true dynasty in their adopted land, and took for their symbol the shamrock.

They were a healthy family, a lucky family, but not invulnerable. War and sickness and accidents took their toll, reducing their number inexorably. Finally there was only a single Delaney son controlling the vast empire his ancestors had built. He, too, answered the call to battle in a world war, and when it was over, he answered another call—this one from the land of his ancestors. He was proud to find the Delaney name still known and respected, and fierce in his newfound love for the land of his family's earliest roots.

But his own roots were deeply set in the soil of Arizona, and at last he came home. He brought with him a bride, a true Irish colleen with merry black eyes and a soft, gentle touch. And he promised her and himself that the Delaney family would grow again.

While his country adjusted to a life without war, and prosperity grew, Patrick Delaney and his wife, Erin, set about building their family. They had three sons: Burke, York, and Rafe.

As the boys grew, so did the empire. Patrick was a canny businessman, expanding what his ancestors had built until the Delaney family employed thousands. Ventures into mining and high finance proved lucrative, and the old homestead, Killara, expanded dramatically.

By the time twenty-one-year-old Burke was in college, the Delaney interests were vast and complex. Burke was preparing to assume some of the burden of the family business, while nineteen-year-old York was graduating from high school, and seventeen-year-old Rafe was spending every spare moment on a horse, any horse, at the old Shamrock Ranch.

Then tragedy struck. On their way to Ireland for a long-overdue vacation, Patrick and Erin Delaney were killed in a plane crash, leaving three sons to mourn them.

Leaving three sons . . . and a dynasty.

One

She was trying to reach the sun before it disappeared over the edge of the world. The hooves of the powerful gray Arabian she was riding thundered over the ground toward the orange fireball that hung suspended above the Arizona horizon. The Sulphur Springs Valley was bathed in jewel colors, the air seeming to shimmer with them.

Beneath her spring had laid down a hand-embroidered carpet of wild flowers. Around her the lush green of the valley rolled up into foothills and stopped, only a few of its fingers daring to creep higher into the burnt sienna mountains. As each minute passed and the sun abandoned yet other creases or scars on the faces of the mountains, the light deepened to even more vivid hues.

Cara Winston laughed, but only the horse and the wind heard her, and that was just the way she wanted it. Since her departure from the Delaney family homestead, Killara, sixteen years before had involved such a private grief, she had determined that her return should be a private celebration. No one had comforted the nine-year-old Cara then; no one would share the happiness of the twenty-five-year-old Cara now.

This ride had been a spur-of-the-moment notion. A little earlier Cara had admitted to Bridget, the Delaneys' housekeeper, that she hadn't slept in thirty-six hours. Bridget had shown true horror at the revelation and ushered her off to a huge bedroom for a nap. Dutifully Cara had stripped down to her lace camisole and half slip and climbed into the big four-poster bed. She had even shut her eyes. For a minute.

But it was simply too exciting to be back on Killara after all this time, and her gray eyes had flown open. Turning her head toward the French doors, she had seen the descending sun, and the impulse to chase it had hit her. She reached for the dress she had worn since last night's party in Paris. The dress was made of three layers of chiffon—crimson on top, then tangerine, then gold—and was designed so that when she moved, the bottom two colors showed like frilly petticoats. She had put it on and rushed out to find a horse with spirit who would race with her to the sun.

Now, beneath her, she could feel his muscles bunching and extending as his long legs ate up the distance. Shalimar. That was what the stablehand had said his name was. Cara had bridled and mounted the Arabian, prevailing with a brilliant smile over the objections the bemused man was attempting to voice.

Holding onto the reins with one hand and the horse's mane with the other, Cara laughed again.

The wind welcomed her, blowing through the long silver-blond strands of her hair and whipping up the edges of her flame-hued skirts. She had tucked the front of the skirts beneath her thighs to protect her skin from the horse's hide, but the rest flowed out over the horse's back in ruffled banners.

Her dress had been created in Paris by one of the fashion world's leading designers; the Arizona sunset had been created by nature. Yet the brilliant colors of her dress and the sunset matched. Nature had seen fit to add only a large swash of magenta and a touch of deep vermilion to the sky.

Cara bent her head to Shalimar's neck and urged him to go faster. The happiness that was racing through her blood verged on intoxication. Killara. She had forgotten how crystal-clear the air, how wide the sky, how deafening the silence. Killara, the place she had been the happiest for the longest period of time. She had needed desperately to see it once again.

As soon as Burke Delaney reached Killara land, he pulled back on the throttle, slowing his speed, and swooped the helicopter low until he was skimming along the ground. He lived in Tucson on the top floor of Delaney Tower and, conveniently, worked in the large corner office on the floor below. But Killara was his real home, and the first sight of it never failed to thrill him.

His feelings for Killara went far deeper than the mere satisfaction some people might experience at owning such a magnificent ranch. He had had wealth all his life, and had inherited the power and the responsibility that went along with it when he was twenty-one. Since then he had tripled the net worth of Delaney Enterprises, and he and his two younger brothers owned land in five states.

But Killara was the original homestead of the Delaneys, the land Burke's ancestors had chosen to settle after they emigrated from Ireland. It was his and his brothers' heritage, a heritage all three of them were intensely proud of. And if tomorrow they awoke to find they were in danger of losing all they possessed, this was the piece of land to which they would retreat and for which they would fight. They had inherited the responsibilities of a dynasty, and each would go to his death fighting to preserve it, as Delaneys before them had.

Burke rubbed the back of his neck in an effort to alleviate the fatigue that always seemed to gather there. A large emerald glinted on his finger. Cut to the precise shape of a shamrock and set into a heavy gold ring, the emerald had been handed down from eldest son to eldest son for over three centuries.

As head of Delaney Enterprises, Burke carried out his duties with brilliance and ease. These last months, however, his schedule had been grueling. In addition to a complicated takeover, there had been the conclusion of an extremely distasteful court case. Normally he considered himself invulnerable, but the court case had been particularly nasty and had, at least partially, reopened an old wound. As a result, he knew York and Rafe had been worried about him.

His brothers had their own responsibilities of course. York was head of the family's mining and oil interests, and Rafe ran Shamrock, a horse ranch known throughout the country for its excellent breeding and training programs. They had been urging him to take a rest, and he had finally agreed.

Burke hadn't planned to leave Tucson until Friday evening, but it had been three months since he had set foot on Killara, and he had been eager to return to the ranch. With careful planning he had been able to get away twenty-four hours early, giving himself a rare four-day weekend.

He eased the copter into a southeasterly turn, heading for the landing strip, when out of the corner of his eye he picked up a flash of color, then movement. He peered down at a horse and rider, usually an ordinary sight on Killara, a ranch that employed over a hundred people, all of whom rode. But this wasn't at all ordinary, Burke noted, because the horse being ridden was *his* horse. Only he rode Shalimar. Yet now mounted on his horse was a silver-haired girl—riding bareback, and in a red evening dress—and he had no idea who she was. Maybe York and Rafe were right, he mused. He needed a rest far more than he realized!

The horse and rider passed beneath him at a breakneck pace and emerged on the other side. Shalimar's light gray tail and mane streamed behind him, and the material of the girl's dress lifted and undulated like a flame in the wind. Together the girl and the horse looked like light and fire streaking across the range.

At that moment the girl turned and waved, and he decided that she could very well be an illusion conjured up by his tired mind. A vision. A fantasy. Yet it had been a long time since he had had any fantasies about women. He of all people knew that women were safe only when a set of rules were laid down and abided by.

Banking the helicopter in a wide circle around her, he motioned for her to stop. He saw her reining in Shalimar and reflected that it was a good thing the Arabian had been a gift to him from Rafe. Rafe saw to it that no horse left Shamrock without being well trained. Burke flew the helicopter some distance away, so that when he landed, the downwash from the blades wouldn't hurt the girl or the horse.

Cara watched as the helicopter settled on the ground. If she hadn't guessed already, the shamrock logo on the side of the copter's door would have told her it belonged to Delaney Enterprises. Underneath her the sleek horse snorted and tossed his head, restless to be off again, but otherwise he showed no sign of alarm at the loud noise and swirling dust.

The blades whooshed to a stop, the door opened, and a man stepped out. He was in his thirties, a tall man, with bronze-dark skin and black hair. All three of the Delaney brothers could fit that description, she remembered, so she wasn't immediately sure which of the three this man was.

He started toward her, moving with a hard-muscled deliberation that spoke of great measures of self-assurance and authority. His thick hair was well-styled and brushed the collar of his shirt. He wore the dress pants of a business suit, but he had undone several of the buttons on his shirt and had rolled his sleeves up over his forearms. Over the years Cara had occasionally come across articles in newspapers or magazines about the Delaneys, so it was all these things together, plus the rough-hewn, almost savage features of his face that finally made her decide which brother was approaching. The dark green eyes and the fabulous Delaney emerald glinting against the bronze skin of his hand only confirmed her judgment: This was the formidable Burke Delaney.

As he drew closer Burke realized he had been wrong. It was no girl who controlled Shalimar with such ease. She was a woman in every sense of the word. And quite the most glorious woman he had ever seen. She sat slim and erect astride the snorting, prancing Shalimar. She wore no shoes, and her skirt had ridden up her thighs, revealing a long expanse of smooth golden leg. If one disregarded her dress and her silver blond hair, she could have been a proud Indian maiden of long ago.

There was a perfectly reasonable explanation for this, he assured himself. Yet, silhouetted against the setting sun as she was, she had a beauty that was almost ethereal, and he couldn't shake the feeling that she was some anomalous vision that might disappear at any moment.

He halted in front of his horse and stroked its dark muzzle. Glancing up at the woman, he was momentarily disoriented by eyes the color of smoke. He knew she wouldn't realize the effect she had on him. He had the well-deserved reputation of keeping a poker face in even the most dramatic situations. No one could tell what Burke Delaney was thinking unless he wanted them to.

"Hi," she greeted him easily, giving no indication that she was disturbed in any way about being caught riding his prize Arabian, bareback, and in an evening dress. "Did you just get in from Tucson?"

He nodded. Her voice had an unusual lilt to it, but he thought he could detect a faint trace of an English accent.

"I thought so." She let go of Shalimar's mane to indicate Burke's business clothes.

"Where were you coming from?" he asked casually. "Or going to?"

With a balletic motion she lifted her leg over the horse's neck and slipped to the ground. Her long hair swung through the air, gleaming in the sunset so that Burke couldn't decide whether it was silver with the color of gold running through it, or gold highlighted by strands of silver. But one thing was for sure: Whoever or whatever she was, he was having the oddest reaction to her that he'd had in all his thirty-six years.

"I was trying to catch the sun before it went down," she said. A gust of wind stirred the long green grass and billowed the gossamer fabric of her dress around her ankles.

"To catch the sun," he repeated, bemused, wondering what else he had expected a vision to say. She was a phenomenon that made no sense, and suddenly he decided she didn't need to. After all, a lot of phenomena made no sense, but still you could appreciate and enjoy them.

He took the reins out of her hand, pulled them over Shalimar's head, and let them drop to the ground. The horse would stay. Then, before he could think his actions through, he reached for her. She came against him easily—just as in a fantasy.

"What are you doing?" Her eyes had shaded to an

alluring smoke-tinted blue that reflected the indigo of the sky. But she showed no fear, and her very fearlessness made him all the more determined.

When he spoke, his voice sounded as harsh as the mountains that surrounded them. "I'm going to kiss you."

"Why?"

"You're on my horse. You're on my land. I figure you must belong to me too." And he lowered his head and blotted out the light from the dying sun. But, perhaps because he was subconsciously afraid that she would vanish, his mouth only whispered over hers, then touched lightly. She didn't resist. He increased the pressure. She didn't vanish.

Her lips were soft and had a taste of sweetness to them that couldn't be real. Yet . . . He pulled his mouth away to see if he could find that sweetness anywhere else. He did. At the base of her neck he detected a strongly beating pulse just under her skin, and covered it with his mouth. It pounded against his lips. He inhaled and discovered a scent of wild grasses at dawn and exotic flowers in full bloom at midnight. A small sound reached his ears, a cry of frustration that he couldn't deny. Hungrily he retraced the route to her mouth and found it open, ready for him. His tongue searched, met hers, the kiss deepened, and she responded wildly—just as in a fantasy.

The sun continued its descent. He felt the air cooling around them, but it didn't matter. The sun had settled its vibrancy on them. Its lingering warmth flowed over them as their warmth flowed into each other.

He could feel her soft breasts crush against him.

He thought he could even feel their pointed tips. He groaned. His fingers wound through her silken hair, and his other hand slid from the chiffon at her waist up to the scooped back and felt silken flesh. She was made of silk, Burke thought—just as in a fantasy.

But she wasn't, he reminded himself forcibly. She couldn't be! She might respond and taste and feel as if he'd fantasized her, but this woman was warm flesh and hot blood. *Real*. He had been thrown by the sight of a sophisticated beauty riding his horse across the wild land. He was indulging himself, something he rarely did. And it was good. More than that—it was great! For moments it hadn't needed to make sense. Now it did.

He drew away, meaning to question her, but his attention was caught by the way his kiss had softened her eyes and made her lips appear fuller, redder. Then she ran her tongue over them— experimentally, naturally, as if she wanted to pick up any last taste of him that remained. Whatever questions he might have been about to ask went right out of his head.

When he'd announced he was going to kiss her, Cara had decided on the instant that if she couldn't touch the sun, she would kiss Burke Delaney. Just once. Her instinct had told her that kissing him might equal the experience of touching the sun. She had been right. The one thing she couldn't have known was that his kiss would burn her far more than she imagined touching the sun ever could.

And even now the silence between them seemed filled with the fervor of their kiss. It would be very easy to go back into his arms. But it might be impossible to leave them again. *Break this spell,* she ordered herself. *Say something, anything.* She said the first thing that came to mind. "I understand that you can't catch the sun. I didn't even want to hold it. I only wanted to touch it. Just for a moment." She looked at him and saw that his rugged face was totally expressionless. "You don't understand, do you?"

"No. I don't understand much of anything at this point. But there is something I would like to ask." He paused. "Do you respond to every man who kisses you the way you just responded to me?"

She hesitated as if debating something. Finally she asked, "Honestly?"

He nodded.

"I don't think I ever have."

His mouth quirked. "I suppose I should ask who you are, but I don't think I've decided exactly where my priorities are falling at the moment."

She smiled, and the genuine warmth of her smile struck Burke's stomach with a driving force. "My name's Cara." Just then Shalimar pawed the ground, showing his impatience with the situation. Reaching out, she stroked his neck, immediately soothing him. "He's a wonderful horse. I hope you don't mind my riding him."

"I was just surprised, that's all. I can't remember anyone but me and my brother Rafe ever riding him before. And Rafe was the one who trained him."

"He's a dream to ride. I saw Shalimar and couldn't resist. By the way, don't blame your stablehand. I really didn't give him a chance."

"I know the feeling." His gaze lowered to her

mouth where his lips had been only minutes before, and he had to fight back a fresh surge of desire. Because of it, he deliberately laced his words with sarcasm. "Tell me, do you always ride in an evening dress, or was this just a special occasion?"

Neither his question or his tone seemed to faze her. "I told you. It was the sun. I've been coming toward it all day. I caught the Concorde in Paris this morning and flew to New York. I had a meal with a few friends—their breakfast, my lunch—and then took a flight into Tucson this afternoon. At the airport I rented a car and drove straight to Killara."

He raised his brows, and in his amazement forgot the sarcasm. "You came through eight time zones and four airports to get to the sun wearing that dress?"

She bent to pick a handful of golden poppies and held them to her nose. "I was at a party last night in Paris. It lasted until morning. Actually"—she laughed lightly—"it's probably still going on. But it paused long enough so that everyone could take me to the airport. We made one quick stop at my apartment and I packed a small bag." She offered the flowers for Shalimar's sniff, and he ate them.

Burke's forehead creased into a series of wrinkles. "How long has this trip been planned?"

"It wasn't planned at all. It was a total impulse. When morning dawned, and it was rainy and cold, I decided I couldn't stay in Paris one more day." She gazed over his shoulder toward the horizon, remembering that the weather had been only a very minor part of her precipitate decision. "The sun has gone down."

He picked up on the regret in her voice. "It always does, but it will be back tomorrow."

"Yes, but it's never the same. People make the mistake of thinking it is, but it isn't. This was one splendid day, and it will never come again. Unfortunately there was no way we could make it stay." She looked back at him and saw the puzzled expression on his face. She smiled. "Let me relieve your mind. I can imagine how bizarre this all must seem to you. But the trip, the gown, even the ride on Shalimar, was all the result of . . . well, let's just say a set of circumstances. It simply happened, that's all. And for your part in it—the use of Shalimar, your land . . . and the kiss—I thank you very much. But now I'll be on my way." She bent to gather Shalimar's reins.

"Wait! Where are you going?" It was the strangest thing. She hadn't as yet moved away from him, but the thought that she was about to disturbed him. He had the urge to grab her and hold her tight so she wouldn't be able to leave.

"Oh, I'll probably drive back to Tucson and get a room in a hotel for the night."

He frowned. "That's nonsense! You've got to be exhausted!"

"Not yet, although I'm sure I will be soon. My thirty-six hours without sleep are bound to start catching up with me. The sun kept me awake for a while, but now it's gone." She rubbed her arms as if she were getting cold.

"Don't you have a wrap?"

"Yes, but I think I left it in the car." Actually it had been he who had made her feel a sudden chill, because all at once she had felt that he was still holding her in some way. "Is it okay if I ride Shalimar back? The rental car's there."

"I think the best thing for you to do is to spend the night. Or even the weekend. You've come this far. You might as well stay awhile."

"I don't know," she said doubtfully. "I really hadn't planned on being here longer than a few hours."

He already knew that she traveled very fast. Now he wondered what it would take to keep her still. "You didn't plan to come either. And I'm just talking about a weekend."

She gazed out over the range and saw that the light had all but faded. "It might not be good to stay. This is Killara, and it's special." She looked at him, her gray eyes wide and very serious. "You know what I mean?"

He shook his head. This strangely unsettled feeling was completely alien. It had started the moment he had looked out the window of his helicopter and seen Cara racing toward the sun. Since then it had grown steadily, and he couldn't explain why. He didn't like anything he couldn't explain.

Suddenly she laughed, her mood changing as quickly as the direction of the wind. "Most people don't understand, and it doesn't really matter anyway."

Before he could move to help her, she had grabbed Shalimar's mane with her left hand, stepped back, and swung up on the horse's back, all with one smooth motion.

She was like quicksilver, he thought. And it was impossible to hold quicksilver. "Are you going to stay?"

"I don't know."

"Then I'll meet you at the stables, and we'll talk about it some more." He lifted a hand and set off for the helicopter.

Keeping the horse beneath her firmly under control, Cara watched him go, reflecting that Burke Delaney was quite a man. His kiss had told her much about him, the main thing being that he took what he wanted. She could just imagine what his "We'll talk about it some more" conversation would consist of. She was sure his methods of converting people to his views would resemble the way a storm moved across the desert, rolling over any obstacles in its path. Not that it mattered. She would stay only if she decided that she could handle it emotionally. That was the way she had lived her life for quite a few years, and despite Burke Delaney, she would continue to do so.

He turned around once and gazed at her for a long moment before he climbed into the helicopter and started up the engine. Cara raised a hand in farewell, then set Shalimar into a slow canter. The sun was gone. She was in no hurry now.

Two

When Cara rode into the stableyard, Burke was waiting for her. As he was flying to the landing pad, he had attempted to sort things through. He knew she was real, yet some part of him clung to the feeling that she wasn't. Dammit! What was it about her that made her seem as insubstantial as a fantasy, yet at the same time a woman so real and desirable that a man could die for her? It was more than her extraordinary beauty and passion; it was as if his mind had conjured her up out of some need he wasn't yet aware of.

Lucky, the stablehand who had watched open mouthed as she had ridden away on Shalimar, made no effort to mask his relief at seeing her return now. "I told you she'd get back," he said to his boss. "I've never seen any woman ride like her. Why, she were like the wind, and Shalimar acting just like he'd never known another 'cept her to put a hand to his reins."

His lips quirking, Burke glanced at his grizzled stablehand. "I've never known you to get poetic over anything, Lucky."

"Well now, I can't say that you're not right about that." Lucky pushed his hat back off his forehead. "But then I ain't never seen anything like her before, Mr. Burke."

"Well, Lucky, I'll give you that," he murmured, his gaze following her as she cantered toward him, her dress fluttering about her in fire-colored waves. "She's certainly enough to throw man or beast."

Cara reined in the gray, who tossed his head, as if he'd heard Burke and agreed with him. Cara was the only one in the area, Burke thought, who seemed unaware of the sensation she was creating.

"Hi," she cheerfully greeted the two men. Then, catching sight of the stern expression on Burke's face, "I'm sorry if you've been delayed from something, but you didn't have to wait for me."

He strolled to Shalimar's head and grasped the bridle. "I was afraid you were lost."

She slipped off the horse in a graceful flurry of multicolored silk chiffon. "I decided to take the long way back. Dusk on the range is something to be enjoyed." She spied Lucky lurking behind Burke. "Don't worry. Shalimar is none the worse for wear. I think he enjoyed the ride every bit as much as I did."

"I'm sure you're right, miss."

"Cara. Call me Cara." She watched as the stablehand led Shalimar away, then turned to Burke to find him looking at her in that intense way of his. She gifted him with a smile that brightened the dusk.

His gaze dropped to her mouth, stayed for a moment, then lifted. "Tell me who you are and what you're doing here. You owe me that—for the ride on Shalimar, for the sunset . . ." For the kiss, he added silently.

"All right." Her compliance was reluctant, because she had the irrational notion that telling this man anything at all would be like giving away a part of herself—something she never did. But then, she chided herself, the thought was ridiculous. If nothing else, she knew how to protect herself.

She shrugged. "For what its worth, I'm Cara Winston, Bill Winston's daughter. I was born on Killara and lived here until I was nine years old."

An image of a towheaded little girl with big solemn eyes and long skinny legs flashed into Burke's mind. On those rare occasions when he had seen her, he had paid her very little attention. Her father had been another matter though.

Bill Winston had been foreman on Killara for a number of years, and a very good one too. After Cara and her mother had left, however, Bill changed and there had been some trouble. Burke had been forced to replace him. But the Delaneys took care of their own, and he had found Bill another job on the ranch—a less demanding one—that Bill had been able to handle competently enough until the day he had died just over a year ago.

"I feel I should apologize, but there was no way I could have recognized you," Burke said. And even if he had, he reflected, he seriously doubted his response would have been any different.

She shook her head, causing her hair to ripple around her face. Burke decided that the color was more silver than blond.

"I didn't expect you to remember me. After all, you were a Delaney scion and I was the child of one of your employees. Besides, the last three years I was here, you were away at college." She smiled. "Well, I better get back to the house now. Bridget will probably be wondering what happened to me."

"You've seen Bridget?"

"Sure." She began walking, and he fell into step beside her. "I couldn't have come all this way without saying hello to Bridget. She was very kind to me when I lived here." She laughed. "She thinks I'm taking a nap. I promised her faithfully I would try to sleep. And while I'm on the subject, maybe there's something else you should know. I'm afraid I sort of borrowed something else of yours too."

"Something of mine?"

"Yes, your bed."

"My bed." The thought that she had lain in his bed intrigued him far more than it should.

"Bridget told me that she didn't have any of the guest rooms made up, but that your room is always kept ready. And since you weren't expected in until this time tomorrow, and since she decided I needed a nap—"

"Don't worry about it. Believe me, she must like you and have been concerned about you, or she would never have offered you my bed. Beds can be made up fairly quickly, you know."

"It's a great bed, by the way."

"Uh, thanks." Normally women who lay in his

bed complimented him on things other than the mattress and springs. Burke didn't think he had ever met anyone as unexpected as Cara Winston. It was time to direct this conversation. "We have some other very nice beds too, and as I said, it takes no time to make one up. You're going to stay, aren't you?"

Suddenly she stopped and wrapped her arms around herself.

"You're cold. Here." He began to shrug out of his jacket, but she forestalled him with a hand on his arm.

"No. I'm fine. The cool air feels good. I think it's keeping me awake." It was his voice asking her if she were going to stay that had caused her to shiver. His voice was deep and textured, like a cool, mountain stream running over jagged-edged pebbles.

"Has it really been thirty-six hours since you last slept?" he asked.

"Thirty-six, thirty-eight, forty." She combed her hair back from her face with long slender fingers. "Who keeps track of hours?"

Actually, Burke thought, he could have come up with quite a list for her, one that would have included most of the population of the world, including himself, but he didn't say anything. She began walking again, and he joined her. But she had gone only a short distance before the ball of her foot came down on something sharp. "Oh!"

"What's wrong?"

"Nothing." She gave a little laugh directed at herself. "My foot just found a rock or something."

"Damn! I forgot you were barefoot." Before she

could protest, he swept her up in his arms. "I'm carrying you the rest of the way."

Her heart nearly stopped. She didn't want to be in his arms. She had already been in his arms once this evening, and the experience was something perhaps best not repeated. She was beginning to realize that when Burke Delaney held something, he didn't let go easily. "I ran out here barefoot. I can certainly walk back the same way."

His jaw set decisively. "There's no way your feet are tough enough to walk on this ground without shoes. As it is, you'll probably have to have a tetanus shot. I'm sure you've more than one cut too. We'll check it when we get back."

His heart beat steadily against the side of her breast, indicating that carrying her weight the distance to the house would be no burden for him. She was tired, and he was strong. Her foot did hurt, and his body was so warm. Why not relax? Cara asked herself. She would be in his arms for only a short while. Then it would be over. She put one arm around the back of his neck, the other she brought across his chest and joined her hands on his shoulder.

He could feel her body adapting to being in his arms, curving, softening, until it had molded itself perfectly into his. All told, he had spent only minutes in her presence, Burke reflected, yet already he knew the sweetness of her lips and the silkiness of her skin. He had learned that she was mercurial, and she seemed to be able to adapt fast to any given situation. *Quicksilver*, he reminded himself. It was almost impossible to contain, but he was known for accomplishing the impossible.

And the thought of trying to grasp and hold Cara excited him.

Her head lay on his shoulder. He could feel her moist breath on his neck. But he kept walking, his eyes straight ahead; he could scarcely trust himself not to stop, lay her down on the grass beside the path out of the light, and piece by piece, tear away the flaming chiffon fabric from her body, and make fast, hard love to her.

To divert his mind he asked, "Where did you learn to ride? You're amazing."

She laughed, and he felt the vibration of it ripple through her body and into his. "On Killara. Daddy put me on a horse before I could walk. I remember mother was quite horrified, but I loved it." The darkness and their closeness had invoked a private atmosphere. Her voice was pitched to a husky whisper, just loud enough for him to hear. His fingers tightened against her. "Then when I was six, he bought me my very own pony, a little brown and white paint, very gentle, that I fell in love with and called Crackerjack. Daddy showed me a couple of times how to saddle, bridle, and groom the horse and then I insisted on doing everything for him with no help from anyone." She raised her head off his shoulder. "The saddle was a small one, of course, but still it was so heavy, I had to drag it along the ground to him. And I had a couple of blocks to stack one on top of the other, so I could reach his back and climb up on him. Crackerjack became my best friend. I told him everything. Three years later when mother told me we were leaving Killara and I couldn't take Crackerjack, I cried and cried until I made myself sick."

Burke noted that her voice held no sadness, only

reflection after so many years. Inexplicably, though, he found himself getting angry on her behalf. "It all seems rather cruel. Surely there was another way it could have been handled. You were just a child."

"I'm afraid it was beyond mother's ability to understand my pain, but to be fair, she had her own problems to deal with. And she told me there'd be other horses. She was right. I've ridden lots of other horses since then."

"Ridden, but not owned?"

"No. I've never owned another horse since Crackerjack. I haven't wanted to."

"I'm sorry I was away at that time."

"Why on earth should you be sorry?" She laughed again, and he felt the same type of vibrations as before leave her body and enter his. His breath caught, and he was glad she was still talking so that she wouldn't notice. "Whenever you came home on vacations, you always seemed such a distant figure. I was in awe of you."

He lowered his head to her and nearly stumbled when he realized he had brought his lips so close to hers. "You're not in awe of me now, are you?"

She tilted her head consideringly, and her silver-blond hair shimmered over her shoulder like a river of moonbeams. "No."

Just the one word. No explanation. No elaboration. It affected him as no word ever had. They were near the house, but he stopped. He wasn't sure he was capable of taking another step, and he had to try to find something out. Angling his head so that their lips were no more than a breath apart, he whispered, "Why do I want to kiss you?"

"I don't know," she replied, her voice as hushed as his. "Maybe because I want to kiss you too."

His already simmering blood began to boil. He had never known such instantaneous need. It wound through his body, coiling around his chest, restricting his breathing so that he had trouble getting his next words out. "Have you decided whether or not you're going to stay?"

She didn't answer at first. Her eyes were on his mouth, as it had moved, forming the question. To him it seemed like an eternity before she raised her eyes to his. "I'll stay. For tonight."

Slowly he lowered her feet to the ground. His arms never let her go, her body never lost contact with his. Her arms were still clasped around his neck. Carefully he slid his hand down her side, past her waist, to her hips, then around to her bottom. He pulled her into his hardness. He wanted to feel her. He wanted her to feel him. He heard her gasp at the contact, and then, with much less care, he crushed his mouth down on hers.

He was like no man she had ever kissed, Cara thought. Her instinct told her he could be dangerous, her senses told her that his sexuality had a violent tinge to it. And even though she had never faced anything like it before, she wasn't afraid. In fact, she wanted the experience of Burke Delaney. For this moment she wanted to know everything he had to give her.

His hand was inside the back of her dress now, his fingers almost bruising. She didn't mind. His urgency only heightened her excitement. His hand pushed across her skin to the very edge of the deeply scooped back of the dress. She heard her dress rip, then felt his hand slide around to her breast.

Inhaling at the sharp pleasure, she marveled at how fast her body had begun to crave his.

Dear heaven! Burke thought. She was fire in his arms. How could he handle this? What should he do? Questioning himself was totally alien to Burke. His life was filled with absolutes and action—especially where women were concerned. But Cara! He wanted her so. He had to have her. Now!

Somewhere a door opened. Somewhere a dog barked. From a distance a voice called. "Cara! Cara!"

No! It was a protest so deep inside himself, he wasn't even sure what part it came from. He only knew that he couldn't, he wouldn't, let Cara go.

But she stirred against him. "Burke, it's Bridget. I've got to go up to her."

"I know." His chest hurt as he rasped out the two words. His arms hurt, letting her go. Hell, even the ends of his hair hurt. "Give me a minute."

"No." She drew in a deep breath, trying to steady her own ragged breathing. "I'll go on up and talk to her. You can come when you're ready." She wheeled to go.

"Wait," he said sharply. She glanced over her shoulder and saw a disconcerted expression on his face.

"I—I tore your dress." She responded to his word with what could have been a smile, except for some strange reason he didn't think it was.

"It doesn't matter," she said. "Nothing lasts."

A deep frown creased his forehead as he watched her run up the yard to the house. *Quicksilver!*

Her legs were so unsteady, they might as well have been made of jelly, Cara thought, but running from Burke Delaney was the first sensible thing she had done today. She should probably keep running right on back to Tucson, then catch the next plane out—to anywhere. But in a moment of weakness she had committed herself to stay the night, and she would. One night.

The house of Killara was an incomparable, imposing, two-storied structure of many different styles and influences. It would have been exceptional in any locale, but it was especially so on an Arizona cattle ranch. Approached by a half-mile long winding drive, the house boasted two unique wings: one, the original adobe homestead of Killara; the other, a twelfth-century Norman keep. A three-tiered Italian fountain sprayed its water in a courtyard in front of the thirty-foot entrance to the house, but as Cara skirted around it she barely noticed the dancing water whose colored lights made it glow with iridescent splendor.

Bridget was waiting for her by the two massive hand-carved wooden front doors. "There you are!" she exclaimed. "I've been so worried. I just went up to Mr. Burke's room to check on you and found you were gone, didn't I now?"

Cara smiled at the tall, raw-boned woman. Even as a child, Cara had found endearing the habit Bridget had of speaking in questions. Now she found it even more so, because it was one thing from her childhood that had remained the same. Something else that hadn't changed was Bridget's hair. A fiery red, it was her pride, and she still wore it as she always had, pulled away from her face and into a French twist.

Patting it to make sure it was properly in place, Bridget waited for an answer.

"I'm sorry Bridget. I didn't mean to worry you. I was just so excited about being back on Killara after all these years, I decided I'd take a ride."

"A ride you say? And in that dress!" She ran an expert eye over it. "It's probably ruined, and isn't it quite the prettiest dress I've ever seen too?"

"Why, Bridget." A low, mocking voice sounded behind Cara. "I didn't know you followed fashion."

"Mr. Burke! I heard the helicopter, but then I thought you weren't coming until tomorrow evening, didn't I?"

Still standing behind Cara, Burke discreetly reached for the piece of flame-colored fabric he had torn and pulled it into place. As he did, the back of his fingers brushed her skin, and he felt her shiver. Desire tightened in his loins. Damn! "I was able to get away a little earlier than I expected."

Bridget folded her hands across her flat stomach. "Well, now, isn't that good? I'm sure you could use the rest." Her gaze switched to Cara. "And you met up with Cara?"

"Yes, as a matter of fact, I did. And she's decided to stay the night."

"Well, of course! She's one of Killara's own, isn't she? Where else would she be staying?"

"Why don't you give us a chance to clean up?" Burke suggested. "Then we'll be into dinner."

While they talked, they had moved into a stately hall. Beneath their feet, an Italian marble floor gleamed; overhead a Waterford chandelier showered them with light. Against a curved wall a magnificent stairway swept downward from the top floor like the train of a woman's dress. On the walls were priceless Gobelin tapestries.

As a child, Cara had never had an occasion to be

in the house except for the kitchen, and earlier this afternoon she hadn't had time to really take everything in. At any other time she would have welcomed the opportunity to view it. But now jet lag—complicated by her extraordinary encounter with Burke—was catching up to her. "If you don't mind, I think I'll skip dinner," she said.

"Skip dinner!" Bridget was shocked. "Now, I'm asking you, isn't that the surest way of getting sick that I know of?"

"I never get sick, Bridget." Cara smiled to temper her firm words. She didn't want to sound ungracious, but she wasn't used to anyone fussing over her, and she didn't quite know how to handle it. "And I think a long hot bath and then bed would be much better for me."

"Mr. Burke?" Bridget appealed, reasoning that everyone knew he had the final word. His response surprised her.

"If that's what she wants to do, Bridget, then that's what she should do. She's come a long way today. What room did you put her in?"

"The housegirl made up the guest room at the end of the hall for Cara, now didn't she?" Bridget's tone was stiff, but nevertheless respectful.

"Thank you. I'll take a tray in my office later." He put his hand on Cara's back, concealing the tear, and guided her up the stairs.

Bridget watched their ascent with interest, and as she did, her rigid spine gradually relaxed. She had sharp blue eyes that could spot a speck of dust at fifty feet, and there was no way she could miss the tear in Cara's dress or the almost possessive way Mr. Burke's hand was touching her back. So that was the way things lay, did they? Well, and wasn't it about time?

Almost asleep, Cara luxuriated in the fragrant hot water that filled the big marble tub. Scented steam rose from the water. She had poured in a whole packet of the special bath oil that was concocted for her by a nice little man who owned a perfumery on a side street in London.

Through half-closed eyes she viewed her surroundings. Both the bathroom and the bedroom she had been given were done in Art Deco style and were exceedingly luxurious. She remembered the elegant beauty of the bedroom with the flowing lines of furniture lacquered a smoky pearl color.

In here the pedestal sink and the tub were black marble, the fixtures golden swans. Platinum-colored bathmats covered the black-and-white tiled floor and matched both the thick Turkish towels that hung on heated rods and the satin sheets on her bed. The wall beside her had a lighted rectangular recess in which stood a tall silver statue of a woman, her hands holding a crystal bowl.

Stirring, Cara felt the moisturizing water slide over her skin. Regretfully she decided that she should get out since, as usual, she had lost track of time.

She never worried about time unless she was catching a plane, and she had already caught her quota of planes for the day. As far as she could see, time passed with or without her permission anyway, so she had learned to enjoy whatever the particular moment brought—until it passed onto the next moment. The other thing she had learned was that you could never tell how long a moment would last.

As if to prove her point, a knock at the door startled her out of her drowsy reverie. "Cara, it's Burke."

Of course, it was Burke, she thought, both irritated and amused. Was there anyone else whose voice would have the power to send chills up her spine when she was lying in a tub full of hot water? "Just a minute," she called.

She stepped out of the tub and reached for a towel. The only clothes she had brought into the bathroom were the peach silk camisole and bikini panties she had intended to sleep in. Hurriedly she put them on, then looked down at herself, only to see that she hadn't gotten herself as dry as she had hoped. Her nipples jutted wetly against the silk, and the top of the camisole barely met the edge of the panties. With any movement, her navel would be revealed. The whole ensemble was entirely too bare. It would never do.

"Cara!" Burke hammered impatiently on the door. "I've brought antiseptic to treat your cuts."

"Just a minute." Grabbing up a dry towel, she wrapped it around herself and secured it firmly by tucking one of the ends between her breasts. It was the best she could manage, she decided, and it was considerably better than the alternative. She went to open the door and immediately caught her breath. Evidently Burke had taken a shower, because his black hair was slightly damp, and he had changed into a pair of thigh-hugging jeans, teaming them with a light green shirt whose sleeves had been turned back against his dark forearms.

"What took you so long?" He stepped in and shut the door behind him in order to trap the warmth.

"Sorry." She leaned over from the waist and pulled the plug from the tub, allowing her bath water to drain and unknowingly giving him a glimpse of peach silk and an enticingly rounded bottom.

His jaw clenched. To his already aroused senses the whole bathroom seemed saturated with her wildly feminine presence. The steam enhanced the sensuality that was floating in the air, opening his pores and entering his skin. His restraint was slipping fast. He needed to get out as soon as possible, but first he had to tend to her feet. "How many cuts do you have?"

"Not many. Really," she added, as she saw his dubious look. "There are just a few, and I'm sure the bath cleaned them out pretty well."

"I don't want to take any chances. Sit down." He motioned toward the lidded commode.

Cara did as he asked. "By the way, I won't need a tetanus shot. I always carry my shot record with me, along with my passport, and I checked. All my shots are up to date."

"You must travel a lot," he remarked neutrally.

"A fair amount."

He knelt before her, placing a bowl on the floor in front of him and a bottle of antiseptic beside it, then he held out his hand. Without protest she placed one foot into it. Looking down at the daintily painted toenails, he carefully turned the foot so that he could examine the sole. His mouth tightened, and his forest-green eyes cut accusingly to her.

"They'll heal quickly."

She had spoken softly, he noticed, as if she, too, were aware of the intimacy of the small room they were in. Without comment he placed her foot in the bowl and began pouring the antiseptic over the cuts. He heard the tiny hiss of pain that escaped her lips.

"Hey," she said quietly, and he looked up. She ran the pad of her index finger across the ridged lines in his forehead. "You shouldn't frown so much."

He was shocked—at her concern, at her insight. But most of all, he was shocked by the intense need that had such a shallow burial inside him that it seemed to spring from somewhere just under his skin and wash over his entire body. With her, control could not be counted on.

"Give me your other foot," he said, his voice husky. She did, and he repeated the procedure. This time he felt her tense, but she didn't make a sound. He finished, put the bowl and antiseptic aside, and reached for a towel. "That should take care of it." Carefully he lay the towel across his thigh, placed one of her feet on it, then drew up the edges and began to dry it.

"You don't have to do that," she protested and tried to pull her foot away. Her nervous system was already close to coming unraveled. She didn't need Burke Delaney kneeling at her feet to complete the process.

The pressure of his fingers around her ankle increased. "Be still."

His command, spoken just above a whisper,

barely moved the mist-shrouded air of the bath-room. Her blood felt as though it had thickened and slowed, but her pulses were pounding at an alarming pace.

Through the softness of the towel, he pressed his thumbs into the ball of her foot, gently massaging every part, soothing sensitive nerve endings, until she was sure there was not a tense muscle left in her entire body. Closing her eyes, she gave herself up to the pleasure that pulsated from every point he touched. Then he took the other foot and did the same, only this time, when he had finished drying the foot, his magical hands went higher, past her ankle, to her calf, to the back of her knee. Funny. Cara had never known that she possessed nerve endings in those particular places.

"What do you have on underneath that towel?"

"What?" Her eyelids flew up.

Slowly he straightened so that his eyes were level with hers, and she could see clearly the deep forest-green color of them. He pointed to the tiny straps of her camisole that she had forgotten were showing above the platinum-colored towel. "I know you have something on, and I asked you what it was."

"It's nothing."

"I'm sure you're right." Casually his fingers went to the edge of the towel tucked between her breasts and pulled it loose. "But I want to see what it is." With a maddening inchmeal pace the towel fell away, revealing the peach silk and lace under-clothes. "My God," he whispered. His gaze roved over her to the strip of lace that crossed her breasts just above their pointed tips, to the lace-banded waist that almost, but not quite, met the bikini panties, to the ribboned elastic that stretched over the top of her thighs and disappeared between her legs.

Slowly, as if in a daze, he lowered his head and placed his mouth over her navel. He heard her moan and flicked his tongue into the indentation, tasting the sweetness that seemed such an integral part of her. Then he looked up at her, and his eyes told her more than words how much he wanted her. She shook her head helplessly, curiously unable to deny him. With an unhurried deliberation that threatened to turn her bones to liquid, he parted her knees and pulled her to him, until her thighs were on either side of his waist.

"Burke, I don't think—"

His lips brushed across the damp skin of her cheek. "Don't"—his mouth touched hers gently—"think. With you and me it does no good. Haven't you realized that yet?"

She knew he was right, and she surrendered to his kiss as his hands slipped beneath the camisole and closed over her breasts.

An ache began between her thighs, and she wrapped her legs around his back so that the exact spot where she ached was pressed against his lower stomach. She was almost completely defenseless and most certainly was offering no resistance.

She tried to think. Why was she letting this happen? She had never behaved like this before. It was her fear of a coldhearted affair that had spurred her to fly out of Paris this morning at almost twice the speed of sound. So why didn't she push Burke away? she asked herself—at practically the same moment she felt herself pulling him closer.

There were no answers. There was only moist

heated air caressing her bare skin, and Burke's hands raising fire where they touched her.

He worked her camisole up until her breasts were bare to him. And when his hands stroked them, it still felt to him as though they were covered by the silk fabric of the camisole. *She was made of silk*, he remembered, *just as in a fantasy*. His attention was claimed by the taut pink tip, and he took it into his mouth and began to suckle. Perspiration beaded on her skin. Shutting her eyes, she dug her nails into his shoulders as shudders of pleasure convulsed her body.

He looked up at her. Her eyes were shut and her head was thrown back. "You can't be real," he murmured thickly. "It's impossible. I feel as if you're going to disappear any minute, and I should take as much of you as I can while you're here."

Her eyelids fluttered up, and Burke saw that her eyes were pure silver. Taking his hand in hers, she slid it along her skin until his hand covered her lower abdomen and the tips of his fingers were just beneath the edge of her panties. "Burke . . . you make me feel . . . a pain right here that's exquisite."

"Good, that's good," he muttered hoarsely. "Where else do you hurt?" His hand delved deeper, until his fingers found the delicate place between her legs and stopped just outside the opening. "Here?"

"Yes, oh yes!"

"I want inside of you. Let me."

"I—"

"You *can't* say no. I won't let you. Not when we've gone this far."

"Oh, Burke . . ."

The delicate clink of china in the next room pierced through the sensual clouds of her mind.

He jerked away. "Damn!" He had whispered the expletive, but he felt Cara flinch. His arms went around her and he pulled her close, holding her gently now, resting his cheek against her head. "That's no doubt Bridget bringing you supper on a tray," he murmured. "It's beyond her comprehension that anyone could go without supper. She'll be gone in a minute."

Drawing away, Cara looked at him. "I'm leaving in the morning."

He noticed absently that moisture had dampened the silver-blond hair at her temples and on the ends. He frowned. "So you said."

"It's best."

Best. She was absolutely right, he told himself, but he had his own reasons for thinking so, and he had almost forgotten them. He stood up, walked to the door, and listened for a moment. "Bridget's gone. I think I'd better say good night." As his hand closed around the doorknob he turned back for one final look and felt his gut tighten. Through the faint mist passion-softened gray eyes were staring back at him. His hand tensed on the knob—tempted, oh, so tempted. But he needed time to think things through. He would have her, he told himself, but on his terms. "I'll see you in the morning," he muttered tersely, opened the door, and walked out.

Later, lying in his bed, Burke reflected on his uncharacteristic behavior regarding Cara. He had always had strict rules where women were concerned. He carefully chose them from his circle of acquaintances, only after first getting to know them and observing them closely. Women had to meet what he considered "safe" criteria, and Burke made it his business to be sure of three things: That the women wouldn't cause a scandal, that they wouldn't get pregnant, and that they wouldn't become upset and continue to bother him when he grew tired and moved on to someone else. Where women were concerned, his head governed and had for many years.

His loss of control this evening had been an exception that wouldn't be repeated, he reassured himself. His reaction could be blamed on the trial.

Burke was a powerful man and, as such, a target. He was used to attacks. They came practically every day, and he handled them. But the paternity suit hadn't been an ordinary attack. It had come from the sick mind of a man named Davis on behalf of his weak-willed, scared sister, an employee of Delaney Enterprises. The charge had been ludicrous. After Elise, there was no chance that he would ever get another woman pregnant. His innocence had been easily proved, and the trial had ended with an unqualified acquittal.

He had come home to rest and to find a bit of solace. Instead, he had discovered Cara, a woman who fit none of his "safe" standards. She had made him forget sound judgment and had given him a taste of something he wanted more of. The damnable thing about it was, he didn't know how she did it!

And perhaps even more bewildering was that somewhere deep inside him he couldn't let go of the instinctive possessiveness he had experienced on first seeing her: she was on his land and on his horse; therefore, she must be his.

So he would keep her here, just for the weekend, and watch her, completely confident he would be able to figure out how she was able to affect him so deeply. Cara was an amazingly complicated woman, but complicated situations were his specialty.

Yet even as he was assuring himself of this, he slid his legs over the sheets that earlier he had refused to let Bridget change. He had known it wouldn't matter whether the sheets were changed. For even if the sheets had been fresh, he would still have been able to smell Cara's unique fragrance. It had pervaded everything—saturating the air, seeping into his skin, working its way into his brain.

Three

"It's good that you've come back home," Bridget said, busily cooking at the stove the next morning. Sunshine streamed through the wide kitchen windows and glinted off the profusion of copper pots hanging from hooks in the ceiling. Freshly baked loaves of bread lined a spotlessly clean counter. At Bridget's urging, Cara had already had several pieces, and she could attest to how delicious the bread was.

Bridget crossed to the table and refilled Cara's coffee cup. "Haven't I always remembered you, no more than a mere wisp of a child, crying your heart out as your mother loaded you into her car and drove off without a backward glance?"

"That was a long time ago, Bridget."

"Humph! Taking you off to God-knows-where, didn't she now?"

"Mother took me back to her home in England, as you very well know. And, speaking of homes,

Killara hasn't been my home since I was nine years old. I don't really have a home."

Bridget whirled around, coffeepot still in her hand. "Everyone needs a home, and don't I know what I'm talking about? I came here when I was but a girl as maid to Miss Erin, Mr. Burke's mother. I left Ireland, and even though my sister, Kathleen, later joined me, most of my family is still over there. But I've never regretted a moment of it, have I? Killara is a place graced and gifted, as are the Delaneys. . . . Now, don't you agree?"

Cara smiled gently. "Absolutely." She had no intention of arguing with Bridget. "How is Kathleen, by the way? I remember her as being such a nice person. She always seemed to have time for me."

"Ach! Isn't she still hopeless? Mr. Burke ran out of patience with her inept ways and shipped her off to Mr. York. And now I'm wondering how long Mr. Rafe is going to put up with her, aren't I?"

Cara chuckled. "She used to make the most awful gingerbread. I don't think she had any idea how terrible it was. I couldn't bear hurting her feelings, so I'd take the gingerbread and feed it to Crackerjack. He loved it." She drank some more coffee and briefly toyed with the idea of having another piece of bread, but soon rejected it. For a person who never ate breakfast, she had eaten more than enough. "I understand that Rafe has a horse ranch called Shamrock."

"Yes, and it's what he's always wanted, isn't it now? It's in the next valley over." She nodded her head toward the west. "And Mr. York is running the family mining operation from a godforsaken place called Hell's Bluff."

"I read about that." The older woman threw her a highly skeptical look, making Cara grin. "They really do have newspapers outside of Arizona, you know."

Bridget harrumphed. "If you say so. At any rate, things are going well, but they haven't always. People say Mr. Burke is a hard man, but I say, hasn't he had to be?"

"What do you mean?"

"Faith! What am I saying? It happened right after you left, now didn't it? Maybe you read about it?"

Cara shook her head. "I would have been only about nine or ten at the time."

"Oh, that's right, isn't it?" Bridget pulled out a chair and sat down at the table with Cara. "Well, you see, on their way to Ireland for a holiday, Mr. Burke's parents were killed in a terrible plane crash. And Mr. Burke, no more than twenty-one, had to take on the responsibility of the family enterprises, plus the raising of his brothers, who were only nineteen and seventeen themselves. Then Mr. York, always such a sickly boy, up and takes off for seven years, wandering around the world like a gypsy. It was a worrisome time, I tell you!" She tapped a finger on the table for emphasis. "And this happened, mind, just months after Mr. Burke's own personal tragedy with that girl Elise! It would have been too much for a lesser man, but Mr. Burke went in and took over like he had been doing it his entire life." Bridget shook her head. "After all the Delaneys who have passed through this world, it has come down to just three. Old Shamus Delaney chose the shamrock as his symbol because he believed his luck came in threes, and he was right, wasn't he? Mr. Burke, Mr. York, and Mr. Rafe form a powerful trinity, they do." Bridget beamed with pride. "They're known the world over as the Shamrock Trinity, aren't they now?"

Cara had listened with interest to Bridget's ramblings, but the mention of Burke and a girl named Elise really caught her attention. "Who was Elise?"

Bridget started, as if she just realized she had let something slip that she hadn't intended. "Well, now, haven't I said enough already? But my point is, Mr. Burke is a fine man. You won't find a better one or a more responsible one. He protects what is his. And if Mr. Burke has a bad point—and mind you I'm not saying he does—it's that he works too hard." She clicked her tongue. "And haven't I told him so, though?"

"I'm sure you have." Talk of Burke reminded Cara that she would no doubt see him one more time before she left, and a tiny thrill spurted up her spine at the thought.

There was a simple explanation for what had happened between them the night before, Cara reasoned. Surely lack of sleep explained the magnified feelings. She had felt as if all her emotions had seeped through her skin to clothe her. And how disturbing it had been to want to hold onto him and never let go! Jet lag had to have been the cause, she told herself firmly.

This morning she was well rested, and there was something she needed to do before she left. Cara drained her coffee cup and set it down. "Bridget, I'd like to walk up to the cemetery before I leave. Do you think that would be all right?"

A look of perplexity crossed Bridget's face. "Why,

of course, you'll be wanting to visit your da's grave! And why didn't I think about it before? You go right on up."

Actually Cara hadn't known whether she would be able to visit the cemetery or not. She didn't often allow herself to think of the bitter hurt she associated with her father. Emotional pain was something she spent a lot of time avoiding. Still, Cara could remember clinging to her father the day her mother took her away, and he had done nothing to try to soothe her. And when, sobbing, she had vowed to write to him and to come see him as often as she could, his eyes had seemed to look right through her.

Over the years she had written him many letters, but he had never answered. Not once. And every time she would ask if she could visit him, her mother always had an excuse as to why she couldn't. The last time she asked, she had been sixteen years old, and her mother was already on her third husband. It was then her mother had finally told her that her father didn't want to see her. Cara had stopped writing the letters. She had stopped asking her mother if she could come to Killara for a visit. She had stopped trying to hold on to people.

Located on a windswept hill, the cemetery overlooked a rolling green valley. For over a hundred and fifty years, the Delaneys had been burying their own on this plot of land. As a child Cara had sometimes sneaked away to come up here and wander among the weathered stones that traced the fascinating history of the family. The names on the markers were like remembered friends— Shamus, Malvina, Joshua, Rising Star.

But today she had come because of her own father. She found his grave in the far corner of the cemetery, marked by a simple granite stone that bore only his name, date of birth, and date of death. Kneeling beside it, she ran her fingers across the chiseled letters, touching the stone as if she could touch him. "Daddy," she whispered.

Some time later Burke found her there, still kneeling beside the grave, a bouquet of wild flowers forgotten in her lap.

"Cara?" She looked up at him, her eyes clouded with visions only she could see. He didn't like the idea. There was something in him that demanded to see what she saw. He waited a moment until her eyes had refocused on the present—and on him. "I didn't mean to interrupt you, but Bridget told me you'd be up here, and I didn't think you should be alone."

"That's very thoughtful, but I'm fine."

"Would you like me to leave?"

"No." She looked at the stone one final time. "No. I'm through here."

She placed the flowers on the grave and stood up. A slight wind came off the far distant mountains and molded her dress against her. It was a soft lavender-and-mauve jersey dress that curved and flowed, taking its structure solely from her body. A scarf of the same material was wrapped twice across her forehead as a headband, a belt was slung low over her hips and buckled across her stomach, and on her feet she wore taupe suede boots. To Burke she looked earthy and sensual, and the memory of the night he had just spent wrapped in her fragrance came rushing back.

He had a sudden need to touch her. He took her arm and they began threading their way through the gravestones. "I want you to know that your father had a nice service. My office tried to contact you through your mother, but we got no response, and we decided to go ahead with it."

"I appreciate your efforts. I think I was in Rio then, or maybe it was Marrakesh. I can't remember. Normally mother would have been able to contact me, but she was on her honeymoon."

"She remarried?"

"She remarried five times." Her gaze skimmed the horizon. "You have to give her credit. She keeps trying. She has this incredibly romantic view of the world. I think that's what appealed to her about my father when she first met him. She had never been to America, and here was this rugged man who was foreman of a cattle ranch. I think he just swept her off her feet. It's a wonder she lasted nine years. The reality of living on a ranch never came close to matching her expectations of the romantic West."

Burke listened carefully to what she was saying, and what he learned about Cara surprised him. They were kindred souls. He, too, knew all about buried pain that could resurface when you least expected it. He frowned. "No, I can see where it wouldn't. It's a hard life, and you have to have a feel for the land to endure. Not everyone sees beauty here. It's too savage and raw."

As one they stopped in front of the simple marker that bore Shamus Delaney's name. Burke pointed to it, but didn't release her arm. "Now, you take old Shamus here. He brought his wife, Malvina, and their sons all the way from Ireland to America because he had a vision. They passed through some beautiful country on their way out West, but he didn't stop until he came to this valley. Here he saw something no one else did, and he was willing to die for it. He almost did a few times too."

Her gray eyes lightened, picking up a violet tint from the color of her dress. "You're talking to someone who was practically weaned on Delaney lore. I remember hearing all about the battles between the Delaneys and the Apaches."

He nodded, then grinned. "Everytime the Apaches burned Shamus out, he just rebuilt. Rafe has Shamus's journals that tell about it. Eventually the Apaches realized that they had met their match, and they decided the expedient thing to do would be to make peace. So the Apache chief offered one of his daughters in marriage, and as luck would have it, Shamus's youngest son, Joshua, had already noticed and developed a passion for her. Her name was Rising Star."

"I've always thought that was such a beautiful name."

"She was a very unusual woman. York has her portrait at Hell's Bluff."

They began walking again, down off the rise and across the field. "You have a fascinating heritage. The pride in your voice is very strong."

"I am proud. Over the years the Delaneys have spread out over the world—to fight, to marry, to travel—but they always come back here." He chuckled. "All but one, that is, and he's buried on

Boot Hill. York, Rafe, and I have a running joking feud as to whether we should leave him there."

"Ah-ha!" She clapped her hands together, captivated by the idea. "A black sheep Delaney."

"Yes, and believe me, it takes something to be a black sheep in a family whose early members consisted of reivers, cutthroats, and pirates."

"Why do I get the impression that the family hasn't progressed that far from those days?" she asked teasingly, and to her delight Burke actually laughed. It was a deep, full-bodied laugh that encompassed everything around him, including her.

"You're no doubt referring to the Delaney trait of always getting what we want."

"That's what I've heard. The Delaneys are legendary for going after and getting what they want." Cara could now see the back of the big house where the Spanish influence on its design was dominant. An eighty-foot tiled pool and spa were here, around which a series of gardens and patios circled and meandered, forming a lush, lagoonlike environment, evidence of what determination and money could achieve. "It must be interesting—to say the least—to be born with special genes for persistence and luck."

With his hand still on her arm he stopped her, and his brilliant gaze turned particularly intense. "It is, and this particular Delaney wants you to stay for the weekend. Am I going to get what I want?"

Her expression grew wary, and a slight shudder raced through her. It was amazing how this man could make her feel cold at times and hot at other times, Cara mused. She had known that he would ask her, of course. What she didn't know was what her answer would be.

"For the weekend," he pressed. "Until Monday. I'll fly you to Tucson then. Someone can drive your car back—today if you like."

One part of her told her to leave, flee, but another part said, Stay: peace is here, happiness is here . . . Burke is here. "Thanks for the offer, but . . . no."

His forehead pleated into a frown. "Why? Do you have someone, a man, you have to get back to?"

She shook her head.

"What about a job?"

"No, that's not it. I'm not working, today at any rate. I've tried various jobs over the years, but nothing has really held my interest, and luckily I don't have to work. Thanks to Mother's last four divorce settlements, I have four sizable trust funds. Her husbands were all very generous men."

"Yet none of the marriages lasted?"

"No. Marriages don't, you know."

Burke had been cynical about love for a long time, but it bothered him that Cara should be also. She was too shining on the outside to be so dark on the inside. "My parents had a wonderful marriage. I still remember how much in love they were and how much they loved me and my brothers."

She nodded, vaguely, almost as if she weren't really listening to him. "I suppose there are a few exceptions. A very few."

Strangely his inclination was to argue with her, but, he reminded himself, his arguments would be only academic since basically he agreed with her. "You changed the subject. I want you to reconsider staying for the weekend." Even as he talked, his hand strayed to her cheek, and he realized that touching her could easily become a compulsion. *She wasn't safe.* He withdrew his hand. "I can tell you love Killara. Stay. You haven't even been here a complete day yet."

Cara chewed on her bottom lip. "It wouldn't be safe."

The wrinkles on Burke's forehead deepened. She was echoing his thoughts precisely, although he had no idea to what she was referring. But since he had no intention of letting her go until he was ready, it didn't really matter anyway. He dropped the pretense of civility, and all manner of jagged edges surfaced in the tone of his voice. "I'm perfectly capable of making it impossible for you to leave."

"What are you going to do?" she asked incredulously. "Ring Killara with men?"

"I can."

There it was—the threat she had felt all along. She shrugged his hand off her arm and took a minute to consider the severe lines that slashed his face into the grim frown she recognized now as characteristic of Burke being displeased because things weren't going as he wanted them to.

She had sensed that Burke Delaney held on tightly to all things he considered his. And she remembered that just before he had kissed her the first time, he had said, *You must belong to me too.* No! Belonging . . . holding on to a person . . . it didn't work. She knew.

"There's something you have to understand, Burke, and understand it well. *No one can keep me someplace I don't want to be!*"

"And there's something you have to understand. I fight for what I consider mine."

"I'm not yours."

His dark green eyes were dazzling in their fierceness. "Convince me."

She met his stare and stood her ground. "I don't have to. If I want to leave, I'll leave."

He uttered a soft particularly violent curse. Her wide gray eyes remained unwavering. Raking his fingers through his night-black hair, he muttered roughly, "Okay, Cara, let's bring the real problem out in the open. It's been hot between us from the first moment, and I'm not sure it can even be explained. I know that I sure as hell have never run across anything like it. But dammit, why not relax and enjoy it? If we're both aware of the pitfalls, we can avoid them." His voice lowered. "It'll be good, Cara. I promise you that."

"Yes," she murmured in the vague abstracted tone he was beginning to dislike, because it meant she was thinking of something else besides him. "Pitfalls can be avoided."

"If we want to." He wasn't used to having to convince a woman of anything, and the harsh strain of his words showed his displeasure. "It's been a while since I've seen Killara too. We can reacquaint ourselves with it and each other at the same time."

"We never knew each other—only of each other's existence." She had heard the strain in his voice and finally decided what it meant. It told her that he didn't know how to deal with her. Her confidence increased as she realized that, unless it was what she wanted, Burke Delaney wouldn't have her.

Her quick, sudden smile made it seem as if the

sun had just broken through a cloud-filled sky. At the sight of it, tension Burke hadn't been aware of began to ease out of him. "I can see now how deplorably stupid it was of me not to make friends with that solemn, wide-eyed little girl."

She felt better, to the extent that she began to indulge in a bit of lighthearted flirting. "Ah, there's the fabled Delaney charm coming out! One way or the other, you're a difficult man to resist, Burke Delaney. The first time I saw you I realized you were a man who was used to getting what he wanted."

"Is that so?" he asked, his lips twitching with humor. Her moods shifted so quickly, it left his head reeling. "I think it's better if I don't tell you what I thought when I first saw you."

"Tell me." She stopped him with a hand on his arm.

His gaze lowered to her hand curved around his forearm. "Okay, I'll tell you, but only part of it. I thought you looked like an Indian maiden."

"*Me!* In a designer dress?"

He nodded. "Arizona is a state formed by the sun and the wind. You have a look about you, like you were formed the same way—like you're part of the land."

She was deeply touched. "What an extraordinary thing to say."

"It was meant as a compliment."

She turned and looked back the way they had come. "It's strange, but I do feel a part of this land. I remember my father used to say I must have the sun in my bones. Even with my fair hair, the rays from the sun never burned me. I just seemed to soak them up."

"I haven't seen you in Paris or Rio or Marrakesh, but here you look like you belong."

"No," she said, the remoteness back in her voice, "I don't."

He deliberately kept his voice light. "For the weekend anyway."

She badly wanted to stay. And where was the harm? she asked herself. She was no longer a heartbroken nine-year-old. She was a grown woman of twenty-five. She would never come this way again, so why not? She made her decision suddenly, as she made all her decisions. "Okay," she said. "I'll stay. But I want to keep the car here."

He frowned. "Why?"

She soothed a finger lightly down the furrows of his brow. "So I can leave if I change my mind."

His hand reached for hers, but she had already moved away.

At one end of the house of Killara stood the original adobe homestead of Shamus Delaney, or rather the final one the Apaches prudently decided not to burn down. At the other end of the house was the twelfth-century Norman keep brought stone by stone to the Arizona cattle ranch from the Delaneys' ancestral home in Leix county in the province of Leinster. In between the two remarkable wings the house tended to ramble.

Cara, with Burke at her side, spent hours wandering through the house. She found to her delight that each generation had added its own touches—sometimes eccentric touches—but added them with apparent love and enthusiasm. The Delaneys clearly had respected their predecessor for no addition had ever been altered nor any purchase removed.

Every time Cara turned a corner, she found a surprise. One of the bedrooms was known as the Red Bedroom because its walls were covered with red wallpaper. Over a hundred years before, the new Mrs. Delaney had honeymooned in Paris at the Ritz Hotel, taken a fancy to the wallpaper in the bridal chamber, had it duplicated, and brought it back with her.

In a hallway Cara came upon a four-foot jade Chinese dragon that glowered menacingly at her, then she passed under a Spanish-style arch that was surrounded by a Tiffany-glass grape arbor. In yet another part of the house a Sala Grande with a thirty-foot-high ceiling and three banks of windows served as a sunroom.

But most wonderful, she thought, was the way Burke regarded this house. As she listened to him tell her about his home, she could hear the love and the pride, and she grew to know more about the real man. The paramount thing she learned was that if Burke had any soft spots, they were reserved for his family.

Burke told her stories about his family's travels and adventures. There was the Spanish noblewoman who added the Gothic chapel, where the altar rail was fashioned from Spanish olivewood, and silk and gold-threaded petitpoint covered the over one-hundred-year-old kneeling cushions. Then there was the Englishman whose love of books resulted in the addition of the sumptuous two-level Baroque-style library that held thousands and thousands of bound volumes framed by lustrous mahogany panels. The second level of the library could be reached by a mahogany and brass circular stairway that was a piece of art in itself.

"You see," Burke explained as they entered the drawing room, "most of the Delaney children were sons, but the few daughters managed to marry and bring home men who strengthened and enriched our family."

He pointed to a miniature portrait of a beautiful, green-eyed, red-haired young woman. "That's Brianne Delaney, Shamus's granddaughter and his pride and joy. She was the daughter of Shamus's oldest son, Rory, and the first girl child born into our family in over three generations. She holds her own special place in our family's history. There are some extraordinary stories told about her."

Cara grinned. "I'm not surprised. As far as I know, there's nothing *ordinary* about any part of the history of your family."

He smiled his agreement. "If there was a war to be fought, the Delaney men went. If there was a country that they decided to visit, they took off for it. And along the way, if they found a work of art, or a particular piece of furniture they liked, they would bring it home."

Cara walked to the mantel. It was made of gleaming white marble and rose all the way to the ceiling. An arch formed the opening. Sitting dead center was a clock of extremely dark wood. "Did that go for women too?"

He followed her. Sliding his hands into his pants pockets, he propped his foot upon a basket of logs. "Several of the men married women they met abroad."

She eyed him curiously. "Have you had the opportunity to travel much?"

"Only on business. Rafe and York are the two who have really done the traveling."

"Don't you ever think you may be missing something?"

He had been watching her long tapered fingers smooth over the white marble, but at her question he looked directly into her eyes. "No. I've always considered my life full. I love my work, and it gives me all I need." He tilted his head. "What do you think? You seem to be the expert on the subject. Am I wrong?"

"Travel is fun and exciting, and you can learn a lot. But after a while . . . I don't know," she finally said, after giving it a minute's thought. Her gaze took in the room, warm and rich because generations of people had lived in it and brought their treasures to it. "I travel because I have no one place on earth where I feel I belong, because no one place can ever seem to hold me." She tossed her head and laughed. "That's not a complaint. I cherish my freedom, and when all is said and done, I lead exactly the kind of life I want. A lot of people would envy me. But sometimes—just sometimes—I wonder if my life would have been different if my parents hadn't divorced and I hadn't been taken away from Killara."

He couldn't think of a single thing to say. It was obvious to him that Cara had been a sensitive child who had badly needed a secure, loving environment. She was a fascinating woman, but every now and again he caught a glimpse of the child. Her sensitivity was a fragile thread weaving in and

out of the stylish, sometimes colorful fabric that
was Cara.

She was a woman who knew herself well, who
was fully aware of her strengths and her weak-
nesses. She protected herself. He had seen it in
action. That was something he could understand,
even admire. But his admiration didn't prevent
him from spending a lot of time trying to find a way
to get through her defenses.

The hours he had spent with Cara had been
totally consuming. Her intelligence challenged
him, her beauty beckoned him. He had learned a
lot about her, but there was so much more for him
to learn. For instance, he still didn't know how she
could make him want her so.

He noticed that her attention had been captured
by the clock. "Shamus and his wife brought that
clock all the way from Ireland to America, then
overland to Arizona in their covered wagon."

"It's marvelous! And it's made of bog wood, isn't
it? I ran across some bog wood furniture on a trip
to Ireland not too long ago. It's seasoned in turf
bogs where it gets this wonderful rich black color,
and then it's dug up. It's quite rare now." The clock
was about two feet square. Running the pad of one
finger probingly around the face of the clock, she
asked, "What is this carving? It's very unusual."

"Serpents."

"What?" She drew her finger away, as if it were
endangered. She wasn't fond of snakes.

He grinned. "An ancestor of mine carved it. The
symbols are from are our family shield—a drawn
sword and two serpents. See"—he pointed to just
beneath the face of the clock—"here's the sword."

"Yes, I can see it now." She checked the face of

the clock. The time was wrong. "It doesn't work, does it?"

"Well, actually . . ."

Cara was surprised to see a glitter of amusement spring into his eyes. "What?"

"Uh, when York and Rafe and I were younger, there was an accident with the clock."

"An accident?"

"Perhaps the better word would be *incident*. It seems somehow *someone* broke the clock so badly, it couldn't be repaired."

"This someone. You wouldn't happen to know who it was, would you?"

His grin broadened. "Mother seemed to think it was one of the three of us, but none of us ever admitted to it, so she punished all of us."

"For heaven's sake! Don't keep me in suspense," she protested. "Who did it?"

"All I'm going to say is that *I* didn't do it."

She crossed her arms and favored him with a suspicious gaze. "Uh-uh. Why do I get the feeling that you must have been something of a hell raiser when you were a boy?"

"You were here part of the time. Don't you remember?"

"Not much. I told you. You seemed distant to me, I suppose because you were the oldest. And I shied away from York. He always struck me as having a certain wildness to him."

Burke laughed. "You got him right, at any rate. What do you remember about Rafe?"

"I remember him the best of the three of you. He occasionally played with me. I think he thought I was lonely."

"Were you?"

"Yes. Back then, there weren't many kids my age who lived on the ranch. But I didn't mind so much. There were other compensations."

"Such as?"

"Such as Crackerjack and having all of Killara to roam over."

He leaned his forearm on the mantel. "Your father was never the same after you left. I think losing you was very hard on him. Why didn't you ever visit?"

"He didn't want me to," she said in a monotone.

"That can't be true."

"It is, but it doesn't matter."

He regarded her silently for a moment. "Would you like to go riding?"

Her wide gray eyes lit up at the thought. "I'd love to! Do you have a horse in mind for me?"

"Shalimar."

"But I can't take your horse," she protested.

"I'll ride Sheikh. He's actually York's horse, but since York's up in the mountains, he has no place for him. Shalimar and Sheikh were gifts to us from Rafe. He has their half brother, Saladin."

"Great! I'd love to meet Sheikh, and I can't wait to see Shalimar again."

Burke hardly had time to move before Cara was racing out the door, her silver hair flying behind her.

Four

Sunday afternoon found Burke and Cara making their way to the top floor of the Norman keep. The stairway spiraled tightly upward inside one corner of the thick stone wall.

"It was built this narrow so that only one armored man at a time could fit on the stairway and so that it would be impossible for a man to swing a weapon," Burke explained to her, a few steps behind and below her.

"How very clever. Leave it to a Delaney to think about something like that."

"I'm sure we weren't the only ones." Cara could hear the humor in his voice, and it pleased her. Although Burke was an inherently intense man, he also had a dry wit that she had come to enjoy. It particularly delighted her when he directed his wit at himself and his family. "Everyone had to think about those things back then," he went on. "Sometimes I almost envy them. Life must have been a lot more simple. If their enemy was wearing a full suit of armor, they could hear him approaching and be ready for him."

Wondering at the change in his tone, Cara stopped and turned. She was probably mistaken, but for a second she thought she had heard vulnerability. "You're serious, aren't you?"

Burke gave her a long, steady look. "No matter what century, enemies should always be taken seriously. And the most dangerous enemy is the one who gives no warning, who comes from a direction you least expect."

"You're talking about something specific, aren't you? What is it?"

She was so close, he could smell her perfumed scent: wild, sweet grasses and midnight flowers. The fragrance always made his blood race a little faster. With conscious effort he shook off his somber mood and smiled at Cara, which he found very easy to do. "It's nothing. Go on up. We're nearly there."

It was his smile that made Cara turn and climb the remaining stairs to the top floor of the keep. When Burke Delaney's rough-hewn features creased into a smile, there was either two things she could do. One: Stay where she was and run the risk of his burning kisses; or two: Move.

They emerged into the large room on the top floor of the keep, and Cara promptly forgot both Burke's bewitching smile and the chilling tone of his voice when he had said the word *enemy.*

"This is a wonderful room. Why it must be thirty feet across! And all these toys! Burke . . . this was your playroom, wasn't it?"

He nodded, enjoying her delight. "It was my and

my brothers' favorite place to play. It was great. With walls six feet thick, we could make all the noise we wanted to."

Cara surveyed the room. A good half of the curved stone wall held custom-made cabinets. Investigating, she found that one cabinet contained shelf after shelf of every game imaginable. Another cabinet held a complete stereo system, along with row after row of record albums.

A marble-topped table stood to one side. On it a carved ivory chess set was set up. In the center of the room a long sofa and a trio of sturdy overstuffed chairs were arranged around a low oak table. As she moved closer, she could see that the names BURKE, YORK, and RAFE had been painstakingly carved in little boys' block letters across the surface of the table. Everything in the room looked as if it had seen hard use, including a full-size pool table. Finishing out the contents of the room were three huge oak toy boxes, each bearing the name of one of the three brothers.

The toy box labeled BURKE irresistibly drew her. Opening it, she discovered a jumbled assortment of toys and books that would be the delight of any little boy. She lifted out a rifle made of plastic, but modeled as an exact replica of a Winchester. "I can just see you and your brothers running around this twelfth-century keep playing cowboys and Indians."

"Actually we had our own version"—the dry humor had returned to his voice—"Delaneys and Indians."

"Let me take a wild guess. Offhand I would say that you played a Delaney."

He grinned sheepishly. It was the first time she

had seen that particular expression on his face, and she viewed it with good-natured resignation. It seemed the famed Delaney charm could surface in many ways. In every sense of the word, Burke Delaney was a formidable man.

"You're right," he said. "Rafe always played an Indian. York, on the other hand, swung back and forth between playing a Delaney or an Indian, depending on his mood."

Cara laughed. "I don't need to ask who won, do I? I'm quite sure it was understood that the Indians could win now and again, but that the Delaneys would always come out on top."

He brushed a knuckle down her cheek. "I think you've got us figured out, Cara."

"The Delaneys as a whole maybe. Certainly not you. You're very dark—on the inside, I mean. I think you have places inside you that have never been exposed to light. You keep them secret, letting no one in."

At her words Burke became very still. "You're welcome to explore any time you like."

"I don't think that would be wise."

"Or safe? Neither do I, but then there are certain things that are going to happen no matter how hard you try to stop them. Come into my arms, Cara." His voice was soft, but his words were a command.

Slowly she shook her head. During the last three days, she had felt a constant pull from Burke. She acknowledged the pull, even while avoiding it. But she was only human. She could offer only so much resistance, and there were times when she wondered if she should offer any. His touch could make her almost forget caution, and his charm made her question her way of thinking. But she would be here just a few more hours, and she was determined to leave unscathed.

She glanced up at the beamed ceiling. "Can we go up to the battlements?"

He could take her, he told himself; once she was in his arms her resistance would melt away. It had before. But curiously he was reluctant. It would assuage the aching need that had been building inside him ever since he had first seen her. But after their lovemaking was finished and she opened her eyes, Burke wanted to see satisfaction and happiness, not regret or maybe even hatred. *He had to buy himself time.*

Following the line of her gaze, he said, "Sure. I haven't been up there for years, but there's a great view from there. The stairway will take us."

The roof of the keep was edged with battlements, and it commanded a spectacular three-hundred-and-sixty-degree view of the Sulphur Springs Valley. They could see for miles, and everything within the scope of their sight belonged to him. But Burke was having a hard time looking at anything but Cara—a problem he had been having all weekend. The designer jeans she wore fitted beautifully. The tailored silk blouse that skimmed her curves so enticingly was the color of the sky above them and tinted her eyes a gray-blue. She looked so damn good, he again questioned his judgment in not simply hauling her off to his bed.

But very slowly over the last three days, something unexpected had been happening to him. It was true that he had had the satisfaction of keeping her more or less in one place, more or less by his side. And he had controlled himself to the point that he had not attempted to kiss her, though the temptation at times had been great. He had watched and listened, and while not figuring her out, he had begun to realize some things about himself.

It was an uncomfortable feeling to be thirty-six years old and only now coming face to face with certain elements in his life that were less than desirable. On the other hand, the fact that one silver-eyed, silver-haired woman could have such an effect on his life was fascinating from a detached, objective point of view. Oh, hell! he thought grimly. Who was he kidding? When it came to Cara Winston, there wasn't a detached, objective bone in his body.

"Your father was right," he said as sunlight wove in and out of her hair like ribbons of light. Unable to resist, his fingers followed, threading through the strands until he held a handful of the silky stuff. "I think you do have the sun in your bones. It seems part of you."

Burke's threading his fingers through her hair was an utterly sensual gesture, Cara thought, experiencing a weakness in her knees. All the more so because he was a man who in many ways was harder and stronger than any of his ancestors. Yet she had learned in a relatively short amount of time that his sensuality ran deep and strong. It called out to something inside her, but instinct told her not to answer. She moved her head slightly and he released her hair. "I've had a wonderful time here. The weather's been just perfect. I can't thank you enough for the weekend."

"What a very polite little speech."

She ran her hand over the cool stone of the

ancient battlement, determined to continue despite his obvious disapproval. "But the sun also shines in other parts of the world. I'm thinking that maybe I'll make my way down to Cabo San Lucas and spend some time there."

"Don't," he said before he knew he was going to. But as soon as the word left his mouth, he knew he had been planning to say it all along. "Stay, Cara."

Her heart picked up an extra beat, but whether it was in alarm or in excitement she couldn't immediately tell. She attempted a lighthearted response. "It seems you're always asking me to stay."

"And it seems you're always telling me you're leaving."

His voice held a suggestion of tenderness, and it made her wonder if Burke could be capable of tenderness. Burke Delaney . . . tender. It was a subject best left alone, she decided. She dropped her attempt at banter. "I have to. And so do you. Aren't you due back at work tomorrow?"

His mouth twisted humorously. "Supposedly. But you know what? It's just occurred to me that I'm the boss, and I can do whatever I damn well please."

"That just occurred to you?"

"Responsibility was ingrained in me at a very early age. But I haven't had a vacation in years. Delaney Enterprises can get along without me for a while. What do you say? Stay with me."

He still wanted her, Burke thought, and he still didn't know why. But he was beginning to think the reasons didn't matter anymore, because his desire for her had gone past the norm. It was now a full-scale obsession.

So that she wouldn't see the intensity of his need

for her, he forced his gaze away and directed it southwest, toward the Dragoon Mountains where, years before, Cochise routinely escaped the United States Cavalry by slipping onto trails through passes that only he and his braves knew about. Burke could now understand the cavalry's frustration, only he wasn't about to let Cara slip away from him.

"Cara, I'd like you to know something. I've never asked any woman to stay here before."

His profile was turned to her. It was a supremely arrogant profile—it seemed carved in bronze—and as fierce and unyielding as the mountains before them, Cara thought. But suddenly she caught a glimpse of the heavy toll his weight of responsibilities must take on him, and her heart, the heart she so carefully guarded, went out to him. "A man in your position must be alone a lot," she said softly.

He didn't mean it to be, but his retort came out harsh and defensive. "I've never brought a woman to Killara because I've never met a woman I thought I would enjoy sharing Killara with."

"I wasn't talking about women."

The muscles in his jaw slowly relaxed. "I'm very close to my brothers, and I see them several times a month. They are the two people in this world I can always count on and can always trust. As for women, there have been more than I can count. Understand me, I'm not bragging. That's just the way it is. But until now, the women I've known have fallen into a category it would be better not to describe. Maybe that's one of my problems. I put people into categories." Turning to her, he smiled and gently brushed a strand of silver-gold hair off her face. "I've even tried to put you into a category. You don't fit."

Her mouth curved gently upward. "But you're still trying, aren't you?"

He shrugged without apology. "It's my nature."

"I know," she said softly.

"You're right though. Great power and great wealth can foster loneliness, and I wasn't even aware of it until this weekend. And somehow it's because of you. Killara is my home and I've protected it well. But this time when I came home, I found you here, uninvited. And . . . for whatever reason, I didn't want you to leave."

There was a long stretch of silence between them. Then, "I almost had an affair once," Cara said unexpectedly. "I thought I was in love—I guess because I so desperately *wanted* to be in love. Of course, I wasn't."

Burke's brow wrinkled fiercely. "You mean, you're a virgin?"

"Shocking isn't it?" She hunched her shoulders. "The day before I left Paris, my mother whirled into the city with her newest lover and possible would-be husband. I went to meet the new conquest, just as I had done countless times before. Mother was certainly the same, all beaming and hopeful. He—I forget his name—looked and acted like all her other lovers: nice to me, besotted with her. And I knew this affair would end, just as all the others had. Everything seemed exactly the same—except I knew it wasn't. You see, this time there was a difference, and it was me." She turned toward Burke, held up one hand, and snapped her fingers. "Just like that, it was as if I had seen my future, and I didn't like what I saw. So I got on a plane and came to Killara, a place where I had once felt secure and loved."

Burke's brow wrinkled uncomprehendingly. "You mean, you got scared that your future would be a case of 'Like mother, like daughter'?"

"Exactly. Over the years Mother and I have learned the same lessons in life, although I will admit that up to this point, we've chosen to handle our lives differently. But you never know." Again she held up her hand and made a dropping motion from the wrist. "You see, it's been like a series of dominoes falling, one toppling the other. Not one big traumatic event, but a series of small events only confirming for me that one can never hold on to anything, and therefore it's better only to touch something, experience it, and then move on."

Pieces were beginning to fall into place for Burke. "Is that it? Is that what drives you from place to place at such a breakneck speed?"

"It works beautifully. You'd be surprised."

"Cara." He grasped her arms to insure that he would have her complete attention. "Don't be afraid that your life will turn out like your mother's. It will never happen."

Her eyes searched his. "How can you be so sure?"

"Because you're too golden, too shining, to ever become so tarnished, and because I couldn't stand the thought of another man's hands on you."

She glanced down at his fingers curled around her upper arms and experienced the now familiar shiver of hot feeling. "With you . . ."

"With us it's different. You can't judge yourself by how you react to me."

"How do you know?" she asked earnestly. "How

do you know I wouldn't be like that with every man? How do you know I wouldn't have a series of lovers just like my mother?"

"I can't explain anything about you and me, and that's a very hard thing for a man like me to admit. Oh, I won't stop trying. But you see, you've come into my life and changed all the rules, and now we've got to make new rules and go forward from here."

"Are you listening to yourself?" she asked with stunned disbelief. "Do you know what you're saying?"

"No."

His admission moved her—and scared her. Here was a man who she was sure never said a word he hadn't carefully thought through first, telling her that she affected him to the extent that he was acting totally out of character. "How long are you thinking of staying here?" she asked slowly.

"If you'll stay with me, two weeks, maybe longer." She didn't say anything. "Cara, I want you so badly, I can even feel my desire for you in the air around us. You must feel it too! You must want me too!"

She jerked away from him and dragged shaking fingers through her hair. *Must.* He was right. She did feel it, and she did want him, much more than was decent, much more than was good for her. But he had said *must.* Through the sheer power of his will he was attempting to pull her to him. She couldn't allow it.

"You're right. But I'm sorry. I'm not ready to become your lover, Burke."

He waited until the sharp pain that twisted through his gut stopped throbbing and once again became a steady ache. Could he do it? Could he wait? he asked himself. Could he wait to bury himself inside her and discover the sweet ecstasy he knew would be there? The answer was simple. He had no choice. He had to try, because if he didn't, she would leave. Drawing in a deep breath, he said, "All right. I'll wait. I won't try to push you into something you feel you're not ready for."

In the past Cara had always weighed all the elements involved in a situation before deciding whether she could handle it. But in this case there were so many more elements to deal with. For instance, on which side of the scale should she put this strong chemistry that existed between them? This chemistry couldn't be weighed and couldn't be measured; it could only be felt.

Oh, be honest, Cara! she told herself in disgust. The truth was she could weigh, measure, and analyze until this time next year, but in the end, it would still come down to the same thing. *She didn't want to leave.*

Burke Delaney intrigued her, and the thought of spending two weeks with him excited her. He had said they would make their own rules—a concept she firmly believed in. He had also said he wouldn't push her into becoming his lover. Under those conditions she was convinced she would be able to cope.

"Then I'll stay," she said, but then moved quickly away, just in case he decided to reach for her.

Burke leaned back in his desk chair and closed his eyes. It must be about eleven o'clock, he decided. He had excused himself right after dinner, saying he had some paperwork to do. Actually the paperwork could have easily waited, but it was best to keep busy. His eyes flashed open, and wearily he reached for a pencil. Yet his mind veered toward Cara. It always did. He couldn't be away from her without thinking of her. And he couldn't be with her without putting his hands on her in some way. And he couldn't put his hands on her without wanting to kiss her. And he couldn't kiss her without wanting to make love to her.

But he was waiting, something he would have thought himself incapable of two weeks earlier. He was waiting and watching, for there was a struggle going on within Cara. He could see it in those smoky eyes of hers that conveyed emotions so easily. He could sense it in the way her body trembled when he touched her. He could feel it in the way her lips became pliant and sweet on those rare occasions when he kissed her, lightly and ever so gently. It was the only way he could kiss her and still remain sane. The pencil he held snapped into two pieces. He hurled them across the room.

Beautiful, complicated, desirable, elusive Cara. His hand went to the back of his neck and rubbed absently. Their time together, if not exactly physically satisfying, had been full, even fun. Killara offered a myriad of things to do, and Cara seemed to enjoy the ranch as much as he did. He had even flown her into Tucson for a shopping trip to augment the small amount of clothing she had brought with her on her impulsive flight from Paris.

Looking back on that day, Burke shook his head in bemusement. Shopping with Cara was like shopping with no other woman, but then, if he had given the matter thought beforehand, he would have realized it would be so. She had breezed through the shops very fast, trying nothing on, choosing, seemingly at random, a top from one store, a skirt from another, a dress from this rack, a scarf from that shelf. They had finished in half the time he had expected, and they flew back to the ranch with the late afternoon left for a ride.

All the activity to the contrary, though, Burke could tell that Cara was restless. Neither of them spoke of the fact that the two weeks she had promised to stay were up. At her request her rental car was still parked on Killara, and every time he saw it, his frustration level climbed higher.

Soon, he promised himself, soon she would be his, and he would take his fill of her to the point of satiation. And *then* maybe his life could get back to normal. Why, he wondered, did the thought depress him so?

Dressing for dinner on Killara was the custom and Burke hadn't changed from the black pants and silk shirt he had worn earlier. He had unbuttoned his shirt all the way to the waist, though, because he had felt unbearably hot. Strange. The air circulating through his study was cool.

He got up and wandered to the set of glass doors that led out to the back of the house. Every night a computer-controlled exterior lighting system transformed the pool and garden area into a wonderland. But with the exception of himself, very few people ever took the opportunity to enjoy it. He gave the area a cursory scan, suddenly drawing in his breath. Tonight it seemed someone else was enjoying it: Cara.

*   *   *

The night had drawn her to it, offering solace from the disturbing thoughts and feelings that were wreaking havoc with her emotional well-being. With every day that passed her nerves wound tighter and tighter. Killara gave her a peace she hadn't known in years, yet its master confused and bewildered her as much as he attracted her. At any other time, at any other place, she would simply have solved the problem by packing up and moving on.

And she still might, she assured herself forcibly. Soon.

She threw back her head and gazed up at the sky. Star-studded blackness surrounded her. On the ground, lights hidden by plants offered illumination that didn't intrude. In the pool the clear, lighted water reflected off turquoise tiles.

Although she had taken off her shoes and underskirt directly after dinner, she had somehow never gotten around to changing completely. Consequently she still had on the silver lamé skirt and gray cashmere top she had worn for dinner. She had added a royal purple fringed shawl, though, that she had purchased in Barcelona one fall. Metallic silver threads wove in and out of it and glinted in the moonlight.

The silver lamé skirt was ballerina-length and full, so that when she executed an impromptu pirouette, the skirt swung out, then wrapped around her, high up on her thighs. The iridescent fabric shimmered as, laughing, she repeated the pirouette until she was swirling in and out of the shadowed landscape like a lovely young nymph.

Holding her arms out, the corners of the shawl grasped in her hands, she found joy in the night. The fringed shawl billowed out, as she twirled and swayed to some inner music all her own . . . right into the arms of Burke Delaney.

Powerful and elemental, he had materialized out of the shadows. His green eyes glittered like jewels in the darkness. "Welcome to my web, said the spider to the fly."

Flushed and breathless, she laughed and turned to whirl away. But he said "No" with a harshness that made her pounding heart beat faster. He caught a portion of her skirt and slowly pulled her back to him.

Burke had denied himself for two weeks, not a long time in the overall scheme of things, but Cara seemed to make normal time alter, curve, bend back in upon itself. Minutes away from her were like hours, and hours with her were like minutes. A need burned hotly within him. There was only one thing he could do.

His mouth crushed hers with all the force of his pent-up desires. The night was clear, but inside him there was a storm. Restraint was a thing of the past. Thinking through his actions didn't even occur to Burke. The aching, gnawing need had grown to the point where it threatened to consume. His need for her would destroy him, and that couldn't happen. It must stop! No woman had ever done such a thing to him, and this silver-haired witch wouldn't be allowed to do it either.

So then why, some dim part of his brain kept asking, did he feel that, when the moment came and he entered her, he would be losing a part of himself?

Burke pushed the thought away as his hands greedily touched her. She brought out all his possessive instincts, he realized. He wanted to burn her flawless skin with the imprint of his hands so that no other man would ever touch her. He wanted to hold her so tightly, there would be no way she could ever leave his arms.

In his arms Cara was not a thinking person. She surrendered, allowing reason to flee and unbearable pleasure to rush in. A sweet, pulsing intensity throbbed through her as he pushed up the cashmere sweater and cupped her breasts.

"Lord, but you're firm," he murmured hoarsely. "You don't even need to wear a bra. And your nipples are so hard!" He took one and rolled it between two sure fingers. "It's like they were made for my mouth."

She didn't know how she remained standing. When his tongue replaced his fingers, she began to tremble wildly and had to cling to his broad shoulders as the magic and mystery of their attraction pulsed through her.

His mouth returned to hers, and he pulled her bare breasts against the hard warmth of his chest. Boldly his hand moved to her hips, pulling up her skirt until he could stroke her buttocks through the silken panties.

Silk. Everywhere he touched was silk.

Why were they still standing? she wondered vaguely. She wanted to lie down with him, to feel the weight of his body upon hers. She started to pull away so that they could lie down somewhere, anywhere, and continue this wonderful lovemaking.

Misinterpreting her action, Burke made a growling noise of protest deep in his throat, and his hands tightened on her. "No! You're not going to get away this time. I'll make you mine. I'll *make* you belong to me."

Cara heard his words in the back of her head as a faint echo that became louder and louder, until her brain clicked back into use. *Make.* He was using her passion for him as a means to compel her to give in to him, and she couldn't let it happen. She had fashioned her life-style of freedom very carefully, and to Burke it was an alien life-style. He was not a man to touch lightly and then let go. His life had made him hard, tenacious, possessive. He was a man other men walked in fear of. She had read about the bloody battles of his successful takeovers of companies. She would not be taken over, by Burke or by anyone. Panic welled up in her. He was a primal force attempting to overpower her, and Cara had to get away.

"Let me go!" She pushed against him, and in his surprise he released her.

With chest heaving, he watched in anger and frustration as she ran from him, around the pool and into the enveloping darkness. He knew better than to go after her. He was too angry, too frustrated. With her. With himself.

He let out a string of violent curses. Just when he thought he had her, she had once again slipped away from him, as elusive as ever. *Quicksilver.*

His hands clenched tightly into hard fists, and the emerald on his finger glittered intensely. He stood where he was for a long time, incapable of moving, his body attempting to deal with the physical pain, his mind trying to recover its sanity.

Sometime later the sound of his phone ringing reached him from the open doors of his study. Slowly he turned and went to answer it.

Five

Because of a sleepless night it was late afternoon before Cara awoke, finally rested. She dressed and wandered down to the kitchen, uncertain of whether she wanted to find Burke there or not. Burke wasn't there, but Bridget was.

"Cara!" Bridget shooed a young housemaid out the door and turned. "I've been worried. Are you all right?"

"I'm fine, and I'm sorry I worried you. It's just that I—I stayed up rather late last night and I decided to rest today."

Bridget raised her eyebrows, obviously skeptical. "When Mr. Burke came in for lunch, I told him that you must be sickening for something, now didn't I?"

"Did you?" Cara plopped down in a chair and looked around the kitchen without interest.

The housekeeper nodded emphatically. "It's a fact. And do you know what he said?"

"No."

"He said to just let you sleep. So I did, but I thought it was awfully strange, now *didn't* I?" She folded her hands across her apron-clad stomach and fixed Cara with an eagle-eyed stare.

"Bridget, do you suppose I could have a cup of coffee?" She didn't really want a cup of coffee, but it was the best way she knew to get Bridget off the subject of her sleeping all day.

"Why, of course! Faith! What am I thinking of, I'd like to know? Let's see." She tapped one finger against her cheek. "What else would you like to have? Something light, I'll warrant. I have some blueberry muffins left from this morning. Now, how does that sound?"

"Fine, fine," she murmured, glancing out the window and wondering where Burke was. "Where did you say Burke was?"

Bridget set a steaming cup of coffee down in front of her. "I didn't." Patting nonexistent stray red hairs into place, she eyed Cara thoughtfully. "I couldn't say where he is at this very moment. But he's been in and out all day, getting ready to leave, now hasn't he?"

"Leave?" Cara almost upset her coffee cup.

"Leave." Bridget nodded, wisking a dishcloth from some place unseen to wipe up the few drops of coffee that had sloshed over the cup's rim and onto the table. "Mr. York called him last night and said he needed him. Mr. Rafe will be flying to Hell's Bluff too, I understand, from Shamrock." She clicked her tongue. "I'm just hoping there's nothing wrong up there, now aren't I?"

"Do you think there is?"

"I don't know, do I? I suppose if something were

really wrong, Mr. Burke would have left immediately. They have an elaborate system of alarms, you know. The system connects Killara, Delaney Tower, Shamrock, and Hell's Bluff. In extreme emergencies there's no need for a phone call. They just drop everything and go where they're needed. It's quite something to see in action, now isn't it?"

"Where exactly is Hell's Bluff?"

Bridget harrumphed. "In some godforsaken spot in the Santa Catalina Mountains. I often say—"

"It's no fit place for man nor beast," Burke finished for her as he strode into the kitchen. "What I don't understand is why you say it. You've never even been there."

"Anyplace with the name of Hell's Bluff can't be good, up in the mountains and all! Mr. York has always had such poor health—"

"He's a grown man, Bridget," Burke interrupted gently, "and as strong as a horse now. We don't need to protect him any longer."

The older woman's expression softened. "I know you're right. But old habits die hard. I've often told Mr. York he should come home, now haven't I?"

"I think you've mentioned it a time or two," Burke said dryly, then turned his dark green eyes on Cara. "How are you?"

It was a loaded question, Cara thought, and she had no idea what the answer was. "Fine."

His jaw tightened. "I suppose Bridget told you that I'm flying to Hell's Bluff this afternoon."

She nodded. "Yes." She wanted to ask if he was leaving because of what had happened between the two of them the night before. Instead she asked, "How long will you be gone?"

"Just overnight." He hesitated, and Cara's heart

lodged in her throat. Would he say anything personal to her? she wondered. What would he do if she told him that she understood his frustration, because it perfectly matched her own? Would he believe her and take her in his arms as she longed for him to do? Neither one spoke. Wide gray eyes held dark green ones.

"Mr. Burke? Would you be wanting any supper before you leave?"

"What?" He jerked his attention back to Bridget. "Oh, no, thanks. As a matter of fact, I'd better get going." He threw Cara a final look, then turned and left the room.

Cara slumped down in the chair. What had she expected? she asked herself. He must be absolutely furious with her. *He hadn't asked her if she was going to stay.* He obviously didn't even care whether she would still be here when he got back. The thought cut into her with the pain of a dull knife.

Cara didn't leave. Instead, she and Shalimar roamed Killara. And when the sun set and the land was completely dark, she came back to the great house and walked its corridors, her thoughts her only company.

She and Burke had led very different lives. He had grown up surrounded by a stable and loving family. He had had a centuries-old Norman keep for a playhouse. His heritage was land that had been in his family for generations. Things and people lasted in his life. Even now, the people he most depended on were his brothers. And evidently his brothers depended on him too. When one of them had called, he had gone immediately.

For her it was completely different. After she had been taken from Killara, she had had no one except her mother. And her mother was the most unstable and self-involved person she knew. She firmly believed her mother had never meant to harm her—she just hadn't cared enough not to. Consequently life had taught Cara to be afraid to reach out and hold on to something for more than a moment. It had taught her, "Never mind tomorrow; it's not even today that counts. It's the moment that's important."

And although Burke didn't see life in the same way as she, he had an equally cynical outlook on love. She was quite sure that the longevity of any of Burke's affairs could be measured in weeks. And she had never even had one.

Since she had slept most of the day, Cara wasn't tired. At two o'clock in the morning she took a swim. At three o'clock she made herself a snack. At four o'clock she put a movie on the VCR. But by five o'clock she was lying in her bed, her thoughts slowly beginning to crystallize.

It was as if she had been feeling her way through a maze whose walls were made of innumerable problems and questions. And she had been doing it blindly, using only her instincts. It seemed to have taken her an awfully long time to make her way through the maze, but at last she could see the way out.

She had believed that she had seen her future in her mother, but she had been wrong. Now she knew for certain: In her life she would not take a series of lovers nor would she have a number of husbands.

There would be only one man, one lover, for her in her entire life—Burke Delaney.

Their affair would end, of course. Nothing lasted. And life would eventually offer her other things. But it would never again offer her someone like Burke Delaney. So she would take this love affair, and she would remember it as a series of golden moments—moments in the sun.

Gradually her eyelids drifted downward, and she was sound asleep when Burke flew home just after sunrise.

Bridget met Burke at the door and gasped with concern at his appearance. His left cheek was swollen and bruised and an angry red cut slashed over his right eyebrow. "Mr. Burke! What happened?"

"Nothing serious. Just a minor skirmish." His eyes darted searchingly around the entrance hall.

"And Mr. York and Mr. Rafe? Are they all right?"

Brief humor flashed across his face before a wince of pain forced the smile away. "Have you ever known a Delaney to lose a fight, Bridget? Where is she?"

"I suppose you're speaking of Cara?"

"Bridget," he repeated, not gently, "*where is she?*"

The housekeeper's eyebrows rose all the way to her red hairline. "Well, if it *is* Cara you're speaking of, she's got her days and nights mixed up. Poor lass. I don't think she slept a wink last night. Though I peeked in on her just a few minutes ago and found her sleeping like a babe, didn't I though?"

"Thanks, Bridget. I'd like some breakfast in about thirty minutes. I have a lot of work to do today."

"Do you now?" Bridget asked, but Burke didn't answer her because he was already bounding up the stairs two at a time. Bridget watched his ascent. There was something powerful eating away at the man, she reflected, and work was his way of dealing with it. And fighting. That was the way of the Delaney men, and she should know. Hadn't she known the three of them since they were just wee babes in arms? Yes, she had! Patting her hair, she turned and hurried away. If Mr. Burke wanted breakfast, then he got breakfast, *didn't he!*

Burke quietly opened the door of Cara's bedroom and stepped in. A sigh of relief escaped his lips. Briefly he squeezed his eyes shut, then opened them again. She lay in a deep sleep, her breathing even and slow. Sunlight slanted in the windows, falling softly across her golden-skinned limbs and touching gilt to her silver hair.

Even now, seeing her, he had trouble acknowledging the fear he had felt since he had been away from her. Pride had kept him from asking her if she would still be here when he returned. Pride had kept him away from the telephone all night. But the question had remained, eating away at him until he thought he would go mad if he didn't get back.

Lying on the pearl-gray satin sheets, wearing an ice-blue silk teddy, she looked so damn sexy. But, Burke reminded himself, she was untouched, a virgin. When she had first told him, he had been shaken. How could someone who could fire his blood so easily be a virgin? he wondered. But the more he thought about it, the more the idea appealed to his inherent possessiveness.

Yet it worried him too. He at least had the advantage—or was it a disadvantage?—of having been in love once. Granted he had been young and idealistic in those days. Now he knew better. Cara seemed to have learned the lessons he had without having gone through that very particular type of tearing, cutting pain. She had been disillusioned in an entirely different way, but she still had about as many barriers against love as he did.

But here he was, asking her to . . . what? Have an affair with him. That was all. No big deal. Right?

Wrong! Something was telling Burke that when they finally came together, they would redefine the term *love affair*. And they *would* come together—on that he was determined.

He stopped. What were the words he had just used? *Love* affair! How surprising. He hadn't meant to use *that* word. Cara certainly didn't believe in love and neither did he.

Then again, he reflected, if he didn't use the word *love*, he would have to find a word just as extraordinary. An *ordinary* affair was a case of Easy come, easy go. But there was not one thing easy about Cara—not getting her and—No! His mind couldn't cope with the thought of letting her go.

He pulled himself up short. Damn! He almost laughed aloud. *Love!* The mighty Burke Delaney was in love! He had fallen so fast and so hard, he hadn't even known it was happening.

He walked to the side of the bed, and she stirred, as if, even in her sleep, she sensed his presence. He understood. She had been in his dreams since she had first arrived. They were all tangled up together, this beautiful, complex woman and he, and he was never, ever going to let her get away.

Still, he was going to have to tread carefully if he wanted to keep her by his side. The fight at Hell's Bluff had defused some, but not all, of his aggression and frustration. Today he would take on some tough jobs at the ranch. Hard physical labor never hurt anyone, and maybe in his case it would help.

He wanted to wake her, to tell her he loved her and to tell her that eventually she would come to love him too. But he had learned that while such self-assured tactics might work in other parts of his life, they most definitely wouldn't work with Cara. Smiling tenderly, he reached out his hand and barely brushed his fingertips across a shining curl. She sighed. Using every ounce of willpower he possessed, Burke cast Cara one last look and quietly left the room.

Cara dressed for dinner that night—really dressed—in a chiffon and velvet black dress. The dress was totally impractical and suited her mood to perfection. Chiffon embroidered with jet beads veiled, yet didn't conceal, her shoulders and arms. From there, silk velvet hugged her breasts and midriff, then gathered softly at the waist to flow to the floor.

She made her way out of her room and down the hall. The house was silent. There wasn't even a sign of a house maid. But Cara knew. *Burke was home.* She had wandered these very halls during the preceding night. She knew what the great house felt like when Burke was gone. Empty. The energy level of the house was depleted in his absence. Now, however, she could feel the vitality and intensity of his presence. He might not even be in the house, but he was on Killara somewhere.

Burke watched her descend the stairs, wondering how in hell he was supposed to keep his hands off her when she looked so utterly desirable.

"Burke!" As soon as Cara caught sight of him, she hurried down the remaining steps to his side. "What happened to your face?"

He rubbed his cheek gingerly. "Nothing much. Just a friendly fight."

"If it was so friendly, why did you feel the need to fight at all?"

He laughed. "I think it was one of those cases where you really had to be there to understand."

"Well, if you're not going to tell me what happened, at least tell me whether or not you're all right." She tentatively extended a finger to brush his bruised cheek. "Does it hurt?"

Her light touch shot through him like an electric jolt. "No." He grabbed her wrist and pulled her hand away. Because her gray eyes expressed such bewilderment at his action, he kept hold of her hand but deliberately changed the subject. "You look absolutely exquisite. That's not one of the dresses you bought in Tucson, is it?"

She shook her head, pleased with his compliment. "I brought it from Paris, although now I can't remember why. I was pretty excited the morning I packed, and the dress is not very practical."

"Neither was the one you wore through four airports."

She laughed, grateful that his anger and frustration seemed to have dissipated while he had been gone. "No, but you'd be surprised at the service I received."

"I don't think I would," he murmured appreciatively, and lifted her hand to his mouth. "Shall we go into dinner?"

In the baronial dining room tall white candles had been lighted. Their flames glinted in the highly polished silver and danced in the faceted pattern of the cut crystal. Sèvres china reigned supreme on the fine Irish lace tablecloth. But for all the formality of the room, the mood between Cara and Burke remained light. Rather than be separated by the long length of the table, they sat close, at right angles to each other.

"What I want to know is, who started the fight?"

"I forget," Burke answered quite innocently. The devilish sparkle in his green eyes told her he had no intention of telling her what had gone on at Hell's Bluff.

Bridget, who was clearing the soup course and who was never at a loss for words regarding the Delaneys, chimed in, "I can answer that well enough. These Delaneys are always the first ones into a fray and the last ones out, now aren't they?"

Burke adopted a wounded look. "Come on, Bridget. You know we have to have more than ample provocation." Bridget harrumphed, and the sparkle in Burke's eyes became more pronounced. "Bridget, you know how certain elements can stir a person's—uh, how shall I put it?—passion."

Intrigued, Cara sat back, waiting. She didn't

know what was about to happen, but she was sure Burke was up to something.

"I'm sure I don't know what you're talking about, now do I?"

"No, I suppose not." He glanced at his housekeeper, then down at his wineglass. "By the way, Bridget, I meant to tell you that Cougar called this afternoon, and he'll be here tomorrow."

Bridget's spine stiffened, and she whirled around, facing Burke with an expression akin to horror on her face. "*Cougar Jones*. Here? Tomorrow?"

He nodded. "I'm not sure how long he'll be staying, but I know I can count on you to do everything possible to make sure he'll be comfortable while he's with us."

Bridget's hand pressed her bosom, which was, in Cara's opinion, heaving alarmingly.

Burke seemed blatantly unconcerned at his housekeeper's extreme reaction, but Cara eyed her worriedly. "Are you all right, Bridget?"

"She's fine," Burke replied for his housekeeper.

"But who is this Cougar person?"

Burke opened his mouth to speak, but Bridget suddenly snapped out of her shocked condition. "I'll tell you who he is! The man is a heathen!"

"That's *what* he is," Burke corrected gently, "not *who* he is."

"And he's a barbarian!"

Burke took a sip of wine. "Actually, Bridget, *savage* might be a better word for him." To Cara he explained, "Cougar's a full-blooded Apache."

The housekeeper stalked out of the room, and in the kitchen beyond they heard a terrible crash of dishes.

Cara's eyebrows arched. "I hope that isn't your very best china."

"Wait," Burke advised, his lips twitching, "she's not through."

In a minute Bridget wheeled out a serving cart at top speed, unmindful that the entrées were clattering precariously on top of it. All but slamming the food onto the table between Cara and Burke, she huffed, "The man constantly watches a person."

"Cougar is president of his own security firm," Burke said to Cara. "It's one of the best in the country, and he handles the security for all of Delaney Enterprises."

"Makes a person positively daft, he does! Those eyes of his—black as Lucifer's own—can make a person feel . . ." Her voice trailed off, and she began fussing with her hair.

Burke calmly began to carve a succulent slice of roast beef for Cara. "You know, Bridget, I've never been able to figure out why Cougar makes you so nervous. I should think it would bother you only if you believe he has a reason for watching you." He paused while he deposited the slice of roast onto Cara's plate, then turned his dark green gaze on Bridget. "Now, since he can't be watching you for security reasons, he must be watching you for some other reason. What do you think it could be?"

Cara didn't think Bridget even noticed the humor in Burke's eyes. The woman paled and blushed all at the same time. "I'm sure I don't know, now do I?" She threw a vague glance around the table. "Are you ready for your dessert yet?"

To Burke's credit he didn't burst out laughing. Instead, kindness laced his voice. "Why don't you take it easy for the rest of the night, Bridget? Cara and I can serve ourselves."

The older woman's face wrinkled with a troubled expression. "Well, if you're sure."

"We're sure, aren't we Cara?"

"What?" She became aware that her mouth had been hanging open. She shut it. "Oh, yes. You go on, Bridget. Have a nice evening."

Without another word Bridget turned the serving cart around and propelled it out of the room with an excessive amount of energy.

Cara looked at Burke in amazement. "*What* in the world was that all about? She was so upset she forgot to talk in questions."

Burke threw back his head and laughed loudly. "Our exceedingly proper Bridget is very much smitten with one Mr. Cougar Jones."

She clapped her hands together. "That's great!"

He nodded. "I think so too."

"So what's the problem?"

He toyed with the stem of his wineglass. "It's a funny thing. Cougar turns into an awkward schoolboy when he's around Bridget, and believe me, there's normally not an awkward bone in the man's body. And our usually loquacious Bridget becomes downright reserved."

"Then Cougar does return her feelings?"

"Absolutely. It's just that courting her has been difficult because he doesn't get out here that much . . . and also because he's having to go slow with her."

"*Courting.* What an old-fashioned term."

"It fits them. Wait until you see them together tomorrow. They make you want to believe in happily ever after."

If only I could *believe,* Cara thought. She propped her elbow on the table, her jaw on her fist, and with the index finger of her free hand began to trace the pattern of the lace tablecloth as she tried to envision what happily ever after with Burke Delaney would be like. If such a thing were possible, she would be able to have love, security, a family—all the things she had never had. *If . . .*

"Cara?"

No, she of all people knew that the concept of happily ever after existed only in the minds of people who refused to face reality. But she could have happiness for a while, and she would take it with all the energy and enthusiasm that she was capable of.

"Cara?"

She heard her name being called. "What?"

"Where did you go? You left me there for a minute."

"No, I didn't. I was thinking of you the whole time."

Under the candlelight the jet beads on her dress glittered, playing off the pale honey color of her skin. Against the black chiffon her hair shone like pure silver. Burke couldn't let himself believe that he was in her thoughts as much as she was in his. If he let himself believe—even for a moment—that her need was as deep as his, he knew he would be lost.

"If you're through with dinner, we could have coffee in the library if you like," Burke said.

Abandoning the pattern of the tablecloth, she shook her head. "No, thank you."

He shoved his chair back and positioned it to face her. "Would you like to go for a walk then?"

"No."

Puzzled, Burke drew his brows together. "Is there a program on TV you'd like to watch?"

She looked away from him, then back. The time had come. "I'd very much like you to make love to me."

Burke went still. "What did you say?"

"Would you make love to me? Please?"

His heart was beating very fast, yet he regarded her steadily. "Why?"

"There are all kinds of reasons."

"Like?"

Before he knew what she was going to do, she had risen from her chair and was sitting in his lap.

"Like I missed you when you went away," she said softly. "Like I want you more than I can say."

For two weeks he had waited to hear her say she wanted him to make love to her. But this morning he had learned he loved her, and now he wanted more. He wanted her to love him in return.

"Like I'm sorry I wasted our precious time together while I tried to make up my mind."

Her fragrance was enveloping him, her silky body was curving into him. Desire wasn't love, he thought, but it was certainly a part of it. He felt her fingertips gently brush along his jaw.

"Like I can't wait until I'm naked and in your arms and you're teaching me all the wonders of lovemaking."

"Cara." Because he seemed to have no choice, his hand went to the back of her dress and slowly drew the zipper down.

Her lips pressed into one corner of his mouth. "You haven't touched me, really touched me, since the first night I spent here. Touch me now, Burke."

Passion hardened his body. Obediently his hand slid inside the back of her dress, caressing the smoothness.

"It seems as though it's been so long." Her lips moved to the opposite corner of his mouth, and her tongue came out to lick at the crease there.

She didn't love him, he thought, but for now he would accept what she was willing to give.

She was his fantasy. She was his reality. She was everything he had ever wanted. He lifted her into his arms and strode out of the room.

Six

Even before he lay down beside her, she was reaching for him with arms that appeared pale gold through the sheer black chiffon. He would remember this, he thought, for the rest of his life—the first time she reached for him in passion.

But as he was thinking this he had to tell himself to take their lovemaking slowly, because if he didn't, he would take her with a ruthless hunger. Already he could feel his loins engorged and throbbing with hot anticipation.

"Cara"—his hands went to his belt buckle—"just a minute."

"Hurry, please," she whispered. As he twisted and bent, gradually stripping off his clothes, Cara watched, entranced. She thought she had never in her whole life seen anything as beautiful as his body. To her Burke appeared as some ancient sun god standing in a pool of moonlight. Muscles roped his bronzed arms and back. His legs were strong and hard, his buttocks lean and taut. He was all male, all powerful, and soon she would know what it was like to be made love to by him. She trembled at the thought.

And by the time he lay down beside her, he was trembling too.

Immediately her silken arms entwined about his neck and the velvet of her dress wrapped around his naked legs. She had enveloped him in silk and velvet and that exotic, bewitching scent that belonged only to her.

Their lips met, and the two of them clung to each other as though they would never be parted again. It passed through Burke's fevered mind that this passion of Cara's and his was a miraculous thing. It had sprung to life full-blown the minute they had seen each other, and it had gathered force during the time they had spent together. Now at last it would be brought to its natural conclusion.

Beneath him Cara's body was writhing, and his sanity was almost lost. But he mustn't rush it, he again reminded himself. He must hold on to his control. Easing the dress down her body, he marveled at the exquisite beauty of her breasts, high and round, their tips erect.

Then she arched against him and whimpered, and her whimper of passion thundered through his brain, hurling his possessiveness to the fore-front like a lightning bolt. She was going to be his and only his! She had been made just for him and he for her, and no one would ever be able to convince him differently.

Cara couldn't stand the torture. His hands were everywhere, softly caressing. His tongue teased, drawing eager response. Shivering with the intense pleasure he was giving her, she raised her hips and pushed her dress down her legs, taking her panties with her as she did. Then the entangling silk and velvet were kicked away, and it was flesh against burning flesh.

Her completely naked form pressed to his pushed him to the very edge of his endurance. His mouth began a tour of her body, wanting to learn her. He circled each breast with tiny licks, taking each nipple into his mouth and drawing on it until Cara cried out. He decided that her cry was the sweetest sound he had ever heard.

Keeping a hand tenderly grasping a breast, he then nibbled his way across her stomach until he was between her thighs and his tongue had found the deliciously vulnerable opening between her legs.

She moaned his name, and her fingers bit into his shoulders. It was all she was capable of doing. She was on fire and burning up inside.

He came back to her. "What is it, Cara?" His voice was rough because he was being so gentle. "Talk to me. Tell me what you want."

"You. I want you so badly," she gasped, twisting beneath his searching fingers that had replaced his tongue. "Please don't wait. I can't stand it."

"Yes, you can," he murmured. A light sheen of perspiration rested on his skin. "Trust me. We're going to do this together. And when we're through, you'll never want another man as long as you live."

Her arms tightened convulsively around him, hanging on to him as if he were her life.

What was he talking about? she wondered with a mind that had been befuddled by desire. Of course, she would never want another man. If she had done one thing right in her life, it was to wait for this man. He would be her first lover; he would be her last lover.

His strong fingers delved—delicately, knowledgeably. Her mouth opened, and she drew in a ragged breath as she tensed, a powerful spasm beginning to take her and tear through her.

"That's right," he encouraged, "let it take you." Frantically she pushed against his hand. He seemed to know exactly what to do, how to apply pressure, where and when. "You're so sweet," he said, and groaned against her neck, "so wild."

In agony he waited until she subsided against him, then he rolled on top of her. Her climax had shattered what little composure he had left. As he had held her against him while she shuddered, he had actually experienced the same ecstasy she had. With all his experience he had been unaware that such a thing could happen. It had been mind-blowing—and nearly body-destroying. His control was near its end.

Her arms were around his neck, her body was soft and pliant beneath him, her mouth was raining kisses everywhere it could reach. She was ready and so was he.

Gently he parted her legs and began to ease into her. He heard her breath catch, and he stopped. "You guide me," he instructed. "That way I won't hurt you."

"No. I want you to do it. You would never hurt me. I trust you."

A new wave of desire slammed through him, and he clenched his teeth. He was having trouble breathing. He couldn't even talk anymore.

He took her hands and laced his fingers with

hers. Then slowly pressing forward, he eased into her, feeling her body begin to adjust to his size, to open, and then to close around him in silken warmth.

Just once did she flinch, but no cry left her mouth. Only soft encouraging words came from her, some made sense, some didn't. The two of them had been reduced to the physical, to the sensory. He didn't stop until he was completely inside her, surrounded by her.

He wanted to pause then, to savor the feeling, and to give her time to catch her breath. But he felt her legs come around his hips and her pelvis slowly begin to undulate into his, and he was lost. With a gut-wrenching moan he gave in and thrust into her with a powerful and primal passion.

An urgent tension built, tightened, twisted, then culminated in a release that took them soaring as one. Their wild cries joined and filled the darkened room. And then there was silence.

Cara lay with her head on Burke's chest. The first light of dawn was breaking. His fingers played through her hair. Sighing in utter contentment, her breath stirred the dark hairs that covered his chest.

"Are you okay?"

His concern made her feel warm inside, and she smiled. "I'm fine. More than fine actually." She rubbed her cheek against his chest, feeling the coarse hairs and the nub of his nipple. His quick draw of breath gave her satisfaction. Even though he had made love to her all night, she could still make him react. Her smile grew wider, and she flicked his nipple with her tongue.

"What are you doing?"

"Nothing much."

"Well, keep doing it. I like it."

It was a while later before she looked up at him and saw that he was frowning. She inched her body over his until she was on top of him. "Has anyone ever told you that you worry too much?"

He smiled. "No one."

"I don't believe you." She wiggled a bit, settling herself into a more comfortable position.

His hands came down to grasp her buttocks, stilling her. "Please, have some mercy! You've worn me out."

"I don't believe that either." Her breasts pressed against him, her legs interweaving with his.

He chuckled, and his fingers began gently to massage her bottom. "Oh, no? Then what would you believe?"

"That at this moment in time I'm incredibly happy. That I think you and I, on this bed, in the house of Killara, must be at the very center of the universe."

He shifted his head on the pillow so that he could see her better. "That sounds reasonable to me. I can go along with that."

"And I also think that the sun will shine twenty-four hours a day for some time to come."

He noticed she didn't say for *all* time to come. Had their night of love changed nothing? Carefully he smoothed a few silver strands of hair off her face. "How can it be that after a night of very little sleep you look absolutely radiant?"

"I don't know," she responded with a softness

and a sweetness that spread a slow burning fire through his veins. "But at a guess I'd say it has something to do with the way you make love to me."

"Make love . . . yes." He raised his head so that he could kiss her gently. "Make love."

"Oh, Burke . . ." Any kiss of his could make her practically dissolve. During the night he had covered every inch of her in kisses. She again nestled her head on his chest, so happy.

"Cara?"

"Mmm?"

"What made you decide to ask me to make love to you?"

"Do you have to have a reason? Isn't how we react to one another reason enough?"

"I used to think it was."

"Then let it be. Let's just enjoy what we have now and when it's over, let there be nothing but happy memories."

Burke gathered her closer. That wasn't the answer he wanted, but for now he wouldn't push the issue. No matter how she felt, they had made love, truly made love.

"Are you hungry?"

"Not really, but I guess one of us should put in an appearance at breakfast. Bridget's already worked herself into a state over the fact that I've been staying up all night and sleeping all day. If we don't show up, she's liable to come looking for us and get the shock of her life."

"I don't think we need to worry about Bridget. If Cougar isn't here yet, he will be soon. And with him here, she'll have more to think about than the two of us."

"That's right! I'd forgotten he would be here today. I can't wait to meet him." She turned her head along his chest. "Why is he coming anyway?"

Burke hesitated. "Just some routine business that needs to be taken care of."

Guilt crept into her voice. "I'm keeping you from your work, aren't I?"

Using the pad of one finger, he tilted her head back so that he could see her face. "You aren't keeping me from anything I don't want to be kept from."

"Yes, but surely you're going to need to get back to work soon. All of a sudden I feel pretty selfish. I wanted you all to myself."

"And you'll have me." He planted a kiss on her parted lips. "There's a board meeting in Tucson that we'll have to fly back for, but—"

"We?"

"You don't think I'm letting you out of my sight, do you?" He kissed her again, although softer this time and a lot longer. When he opened his eyes, he saw that her gray eyes looked as if they had been drenched in morning dew. His voice came out on a ragged breath. "I'm not saying things won't crop up that I'll have to take care of. But I am promising you that there will be time for us. A lot of time."

When they finally made it down to breakfast, it was lunchtime. Cara entered the kitchen in front of Burke and then stopped in her tracks. The most amazing man she had ever seen was sitting at the kitchen table. He was big, massively built and, she gauged, somewhere in his midfifties. His white western shirt stretched across his immense shoulders, and his black pants revealed bulging muscles unusual in a man of his age. His skin was a deep red-clay color that reflected his Indian ancestry. A black, flat-crowned hat with a turquoise-and-silver headband was resting on the table beside him.

He was indeed a remarkable man, managing to convey both a stately dignity and an untamed air. But if Cara had been pressed to pick out the one thing that was the most extraordinary about him she would have to say it was his hair. It was full, salt and pepper, and hung to within two inches of his waist.

He had been watching Bridget's back with considerable enjoyment, but as soon as Cara came into the room, followed by Burke, his night-dark eyes switched to them, alert and ready.

"Cougar!" Burke advanced into the room, his hand held out. "It's good to see you."

"Burke." Cougar rose and met Burke's hand with his own.

"Have you been here long?"

"A couple of hours. Bridget's been nice enough to keep me company."

Bridget's face reddened, and Cougar's lips twisted into a grin. Cara noticed that the shirt-waist dress Bridget had chosen to wear today was nicer than what she usually wore while working around the house.

Burke reached for Cara and drew her to his side. "Cara, this is Cougar Jones. Cougar, this is Cara Winston."

She offered her hand while smiling warmly. "I'm glad to meet you. I've heard a lot about you."

His gaze slid to Bridget, who was busy wiping down a spotless counter. "I'll bet."

"Let's sit down," Burke suggested. "Cara and I are starved, and you can tell us all about your trip here while we eat."

"I can sum that up in one word," Cougar muttered, as the three of them sat down at the table, "terrible."

Bridget brought two cups of coffee to the table and placed them in front of Cara and Burke. Then she smoothed her apron over her stomach and stared fixedly at the opposite wall.

"Cougar hates flying of any kind," Burke explained to Cara. "He believes a man's feet should be placed firmly on the ground at all times."

"Except, of course, when he's in bed," Cougar said unexpectedly, causing Bridget to wheel away from the table and to become engrossed in making a fresh pot of coffee.

"Why this is a charming bouquet of violets on the table," Cara exclaimed. "I don't remember seeing any violets on the ranch. Where did they come from?"

With her back to the group, Bridget mumbled something.

"What was that?" Burke asked.

The housekeeper turned around, but she looked everywhere but at the three people sitting at the table. "Cougar brought them to me."

"How thoughtful." Cara switched her attention to the big man sitting across from her and noticed that a deep stain of color had risen along his cheekbones. He had also taken a sudden interest in his coffee cup, studying it with apparent absorption. "Cougar is a very unusual name. Is that your given name or is it a nickname?"

"A nickname."

Cougar obviously wasn't the talkative type, so Cara turned to Burke for a fuller explanation.

He exchanged a congenial glance with Cougar. "As a boy he lived on a reservation here in Arizona, and that's where he was given the nickname, but if you can get the true story out of him, you're doing better than a lot of people."

Cougar smiled enigmatically.

"I can't stand it," she exclaimed. "How did you get the name Cougar?"

Cougar remained silent, so Burke went on. "Legend has it that when he was just a boy, he disappeared up into the hills. Several days later he came down out of the hills wearing a cougar skin and claw marks on his face and body. But he never told anyone what happened."

Three heads swiveled toward the impassive Cougar, and there was an expectant silence. With a perfectly straight face, yet with the merest suggestion of a twinkle in his dark eyes, he murmured, "The cat picked the wrong day to jump me. I was in a bad mood."

Cara stared, then burst out laughing. "That's wonderful!"

Bridget looked as if she, too, wanted to laugh, but made do with a quick half smile. "What can I get you to eat, Mr. Burke? Breakfast or lunch?"

Burke deferred to Cara with a questioning raise of his eyebrows.

"I don't care what it is, but I want a lot of it. I'm starved!"

They settled down to companionable conversation with Bridget eventually unbending enough to join in now and then. It was Cougar who finally suggested that he and Burke needed to talk. Reluctantly Burke agreed.

He drew Cara to one side and spoke softly. "This won't take long. "I'll meet you in a hour, and we'll go for a ride."

She stood on her tiptoes and kissed him. "I'll be waiting."

Cara never knew an hour could be so long. It was a new experience for her, wanting to be with someone so badly. Unpracticed as she was in the art of sharing intimacies, she supposed she should have felt awkward in Burke's presence. But she didn't. After hours and hours spent in his arms, she wanted only to spend more of them there. Being held closely, sharing words in the darkness—it had all been an experience that transcended anything she had ever imagined.

And now she had lost track of time. She had no idea whether a half hour or an hour had passed, and she didn't care. Impatience, wanting to be with Burke again, made her footsteps quicker than usual. But as the heels of her boots clicked across the back patio and she drew closer to his study, raised voices that she recognized as Burke's and Cougar's stopped her in her tracks.

"Dammit, Burke! You pay me remarkably well for my expertise. Let me do my job."

"I won't have Killara turned into a fortress!"

"I haven't. I've just taken reasonable precautions."

"I won't be *guarded*!"

Cougar's voice carried intensity. "This man is dangerous, Burke."

Cara heard an expletive that made her wince.

"He's been sending me notes for weeks and nothing's happened yet, has it?"

"The notes have become more and more threatening. I've looked into his background. He was a demolitions expert when he was in the service and he's an expert marksman. Put those facts together with the knowledge that he's crazy as hell, and you've got yourself a whole lot of trouble."

"Cougar, I've handled trouble all my life, as have my brothers. You know better than anyone that my brothers and I have been targets for this type of thing before. It goes with the Delaney name and position."

"Dammit, Burke. I wish you would take this seriously!"

"I do, and believe me, I appreciate your dedication to me. It's just that right now Cara is my main concern. I don't want her to be frightened if she notices the added security measures. Besides, we both know that if Davis wants me badly enough, he's going to get through any defense you've got set up. So what's the point? If—and I stress the word *if*—he makes a move, I'll handle it."

"Just exactly what is it that you'll handle?"

Burke swung around toward the glass doors. "Cara! How long have you been there?"

"Long enough. What's all this about?"

Cougar spoke up. "If you'll excuse me, I've got some things I need to check on."

Burke waited until Cougar left the room, then walked around his desk and settled his hips on one corner of it. "I'm sorry you overheard that, but it's really nothing to concern yourself about."

"Suppose you tell me and let me be the judge of whether or not I should be concerned."

His eyebrows rose and his eyes twinkled. "Stubborn lady."

She sat down in a chair in front of him and crossed her legs. "Very."

He sighed. "Okay, but I warn you. It's not a pretty story."

"I can take it."

"A few months back a young girl who worked in the typing pool of Delaney Enterprises became pregnant. She wasn't married, and when she told her brother, I gather he came down on her like a ton of bricks. Enough to scare her out of her wits. He demanded to know who the father was and made all sorts of threats both at her and at the unknown father. At any rate, as I understand it, in her panic she decided to name as the father someone so powerful, her brother would be unable to touch him: me. She was even creative enough to tell him that we met for our little trysts in the Delaney Tower gym in the middle of the afternoon when everyone else was at work. I suppose she thought an added detail or two would give her story more believability, and he would drop it."

"That's terrible."

"Tell me about it! The case went to court and of course, I was exonerated. But the brother seems to have some sort of unnatural attachment to his sister. My guess is that he was unstable before, but his sister's pregnancy drove him right over the edge. After the trial the girl ran away. Now I'm all he has left to vent his wrath on. He's refused to accept the court's verdict and has been sending me threatening notes ever since."

"And Cougar thinks you should pay attention to them."

He grinned. "Cougar takes his job too seriously."

"You're making it hard for him to do his job, Burke! Why don't you let him do it?"

He reached for her and drew her out of her chair to him. "Because I don't want this to interfere with us."

She framed his face with her hands, and even though she knew he had shaved just a little while before, she could feel the scratchy beginnings of his beard. She remembered how its roughness had caressed her own skin during the night. He had apologized, but she hadn't minded. "What would really interfere is if something happened to you."

"Nothing is going to happen to me."

She almost smiled at his unconscious arrogance. "Burke, whatever precautions Cougar thinks you should take, we need to go along with them. It'll be worth it in the long run."

His dark green eyes studied her for a moment. "You're really worried about me, aren't you?" he asked with wonder.

"Of course I am!"

He gathered her to him. "All right then. I'll tell Cougar he can do whatever he wants, as long as it's not too restrictive."

Cara came up out of a dream and for a moment was disoriented. She tried to move her head, but found her hair caught. She opened her eyes and realized that she was snuggled securely against the solid form of Burke. His arm held her tightly to him, and her head rested in the crook of his shoulder so that her hair was trapped beneath him.

It was Thursday, and she had been on Killara for

three weeks. It didn't seem possible. Neither did the fact that she and Burke had been lovers for a week, until she recalled the sweetness of their lovemaking during the night. That had been very real.

She had finally allowed Burke to have one of his men drive her rental car back to Tucson. It had seemed important to him and so she had given in. Funny.

She should try to go back to sleep, she told herself, but she knew the effort would be useless. It wouldn't be long until dawn, and lately she had found it impossible to sleep once the sun was up. Strange how the rhythms of her body seemed to respond to the sun . . . and to Burke. Two natural forces, with Burke the more powerful of the two.

Suddenly a shrill, piercing alarm penetrated the stillness of the bedroom. Burke awakened instantly, and within seconds was across the room, checking the state-of the-art control device that indicated a crisis somewhere within the Delaney empire.

One glance told him what he needed to know. "Damn! It's Shamrock." He reached for his pants. "Cara, press the number ten on the phone and tell whoever answers to have the helicopter warmed up. I'm flying to Shamrock."

"What's wrong?"

"I don't know." He was already stepping into his boots, but he paused to throw her a reassuring glance. "I'm sure there's nothing to worry about. Rafe probably decided to throw a party."

"A party! At this hour?"

"You don't know Rafe."

"Stop trying to protect me, Burke. Bridget told me those alarms meant definite trouble."

He walked over to her. "The point is, sweetheart, I don't want you worrying." He bent down and dropped a firm kiss on her lips. "I'll be back as soon as I can. Now, make that call for me and then go back to sleep. Promise?"

Reluctantly she nodded. He rewarded her with a smile, grabbed a shirt, and left the room.

Cara made the call, then lay in bed a long time, staring at the ceiling. Sleep refused to return. Finally she got up and dressed. By the time she walked into the kitchen, Bridget and Cougar were already there. One look told her that Cougar wasn't happy.

"Cougar, shouldn't you have gone to Shamrock with Burke?"

"He told me to stay here."

"You should have talked to him, convinced him."

Bridget set a hot cup of coffee in front of Cara, then joined them at the table.

"Burke is a little hard to talk to when he's on a dead run." Cougar had no intention of telling her that he, too, felt as though he should have gone with Burke. There had been a brief argument between the two of them, but it hadn't taken long for Burke to win. He always won, Cougar thought with a mixture of exasperation and respect. "Besides, I would have only been in the way. When the Delaney brothers are together, they're practically unconquerable."

"Oh, honestly!" she exclaimed in disgust. "What is it with these three brothers? This is the second time Burke has run off to help one or the other of his brothers. Are constant emergencies the norm with them?"

Still trying to ease Cara's mind, Cougar grinned. "It's a little hard for people to understand. I sometimes think they create emergencies just so they can see one another more often."

Cara wasn't fooled. "You're just trying to make me feel better."

"You'll understand what I mean when you see them together."

"I hope I get the opportunity." She looked down into her coffee cup, thinking how fast her time with Burke seemed to be passing.

"You will," Cougar insisted, misinterpreting her response. "Burke can take care of himself."

"Would you like some breakfast, Cara?" Bridget asked.

"No, I don't think so."

"You should eat," the older woman said firmly, "then maybe take a nap." She appealed to Cougar. "She doesn't sleep nearly enough, now does she?"

His dark eyes took on a twinkle. "Maybe she's found something she likes to do better."

Bridget's face colored a flaming red, right up to the roots of her hair.

"Would you two mind not discussing me as if I weren't here?"

"I'm sorry, Cara, but I can't resist teasing Bridget. I've never seen a woman blush quite as prettily as Bridget."

"Prettily?" Bridget harrumphed. "If you're not full of the blarney, Mr. Jones, then I have never known anyone who was, have I now?"

"I'll leave," Cara said.

"No!"

"No, don't leave," Cougar said, agreeing with Bridget. "It'll probably be some time before we hear anything. Why don't you go for a ride? Or a swim?"

"No."

Cougar shook his head in a helpless gesture, causing his hair to fan out over his shoulders, then settle back down. "Listen, Cara. Burke paused only long enough to tell me that I was to watch out for you and see that you didn't worry. Now, that was important to him, and I intend to do just what he told me to do. The best way I know is to keep you busy. So if you're not going to eat or ride or swim, what would you like to do?"

Wide gray eyes turned on Cougar. "Wait for Burke."

His jaw clenched in frustration. *Women!* Would he ever understand them?

Bridget didn't like to see Cougar so upset. She intervened. "Cara, there's something else you could do. It might be a good time to walk over to the ranch business office. Mr. Burke asked them to check and see if they kept any of your da's belongings, and it turned out they did."

"They have some things of my dad's? Why didn't Burke tell me about this?"

"Mr. Burke didn't want to mention it to you until he knew for sure the office had kept them. He didn't want you to be disappointed, now did he? I'm sure he would have told you this morning but for the emergency at Shamrock."

"But what could the office have?"

"I'm not sure. I'm not even sure if Mr. Burke would approve of me telling you this while he's away, but I reason that you need something to get your mind off what's going on at Shamrock, and this is as good as anything, now isn't it?"

Cara wasn't sure about that and remained silent.

Bridget took her hand. "I can imagine how you must feel, can't I? Your da, he just couldn't stand losing you and your mother. And he went through a lot of changes after you left, none of them good. But I know for a fact that he loved you, now don't I?"

"No," Cara said quietly. "That's not right, Bridget. He didn't love me."

"Why, of course, he did!" Bridget exclaimed, quite shocked. "What are you talking about? Didn't I use to visit him, there in his last days when he was so sick? And didn't I listen over and over again to what a grand young lady you must be? He was very proud of you, you know."

"But that doesn't make any sense!"

"Why don't I walk you over to the office?" Cougar suggested. "Let's see what they've kept."

The office was situated in a modern building very near the stables. All of the ranch's operations were computerized and controlled from here. As they stepped inside, Cara remembered the day Burke had shown her around the offices. He had laughed and said, "I sometimes wonder what old Shamus would say if he could see Killara now." There had been pride in his voice . . . and strength. She wished he were here with her now.

At the sound of their entrance an extremely efficient-looking young man ambled in from an adjoining office. Cara recalled that Burke had

introduced him to her as Steven Whitehead. Burke
had confided that Steven had a master's degree in
business administration from M.I.T., but that he
had never been happy with corporate life in the big
city. As soon as the job of business manager for
Killara had come open, Burke had transferred him
from the administrative offices of Delaney Enterprises on the eighteenth floor of Delaney Tower to
the ranch. It was an arrangement that had turned
out to suit both parties extremely well.

"Good morning, Cara. How nice to see you
again." His gaze switched to Cougar, and his smile
immediately faded. It took a brave man to smile at
Cougar Jones unless you knew him well. "Mr.
Jones. Can I help you?"

As usual, Cougar spared no words in getting
right to the point. "We understand that you have
some belongings of Cara's father here. She would
like to see them."

"Oh, certainly. Cara, why don't you take a seat at
the desk over there"—he pointed toward the corner
of the room—"and I'll bring the box out for you."

"She'll need privacy."

Steven looked as if Cougar had taken two inches
of skin off his back with his deadly quiet words.
"Of course. I should have thought of it myself.
Cara, you're welcome to use my office. Just go on
in and make yourself comfortable and I'll bring the
box in to you."

A few minutes later Cara was sitting alone, staring at a medium-sized cardboard box. Not very big
when she considered it was all that was left of a
man's life—her father's life. Carefully she lifted the
lid from the box and set it aside. Her eyebrows
came together in a puzzled frown. She didn't know

what she had expected to find, but certainly not letters.

There were two stacks, and each stack was tied with a piece of string. She lifted one stack out and saw that her handwriting appeared on the first envelope. Flipping through them, she saw that they were all the letters she had written to him over the years.

With trembling fingers she untied the string and spread the envelopes out. They had turned yellow with the years. Fumbling, she reached into one of the envelopes and drew out the letter. The thin sheets of paper had been folded and refolded so many times, in certain places the words written on them had begun to fade. Her words. The words she had thought her father had read once at most and then thrown away. There had even been times when she had wondered if he had read them at all.

She put the one stack of letters aside and reached for the other. These were written in her father's heavy scrawl, and her heart nearly ceased its beating when she realized what they were. They were his answers to her letters.

Slowly she began to read, and the long years of separation rolled away as she listened to her father tell her of his loneliness and pain. In his own words she heard him tell her how much she missed her, how much he wanted to see her, but that he felt it was best that she stay in Europe with her mother. He wrote that he didn't want to expose her to his agony over the divorce. Just because he hadn't been able to accept it didn't mean he didn't want her to, he said. She had a new, better life, and he wanted her to remember him always as the happy, healthy man he had been when the three of them had lived together on Killara.

Something wet hit her hand, and she realized tears were streaming down her face. She dashed them away with the palm of her hand and reached for more of his letters and discovered the Christmas and birthday cards he had bought for her every year until he had died. The stamped, addressed envelopes showed her how much he must have wanted to be able to mail them to her. Private demons had kept him from it. She knew all about demons.

"Oh, Daddy," she cried softly. "If only I had known. If only I had understood. I would have tried harder. I would have."

Her hands ran caressingly over the scrawled words. Surrounded by her father's letters, she wasn't even aware of time passing until the door of the office opened and Burke walked in, and then she realized that she must have been there for hours.

In an instinctive reaction Cara flew into his arms. "I'm so glad you're home!"

"You've been crying," he murmured, holding her to him with a fierce protectiveness. "They shouldn't have showed you your father's things until I got back."

"It's all right." She raised tear-drenched eyes to him. "Really. It was something I had to face alone." She pulled back and for the first time took in his appearance. Lines of strain had been etched into his face during the hours they had been apart, and his clothes were blackened and smelled of smoke. "Are you okay? Your clothes! What happened at Shamrock?"

"Everything's fine. I'll tell you about it later. Right now I want to know what's happened with you." As he talked, he led her to the leather couch that sat along one wall of the office. He was aware that he was scowling, but he didn't even try to stop. It was totally unacceptable to him that Cara should be crying.

"Burke, my father loved me. He really loved me! He wrote me and told me so, it's just that he never mailed the letters."

"Why not?"

"You'd have to read the letters to completely understand. They show his deterioration, both physically and mentally. And by the way, they also talk about what you did for him, keeping him on when someone else would have fired him."

"Don't give me credit where it's not due, Cara. I would have done the same for any longtime employee."

"That doesn't lessen what you did for him. And it speaks very loudly about the type of man you are." She had too much on her mind to sit still. She jumped up and walked to the window. "I only wish I could have done something for him. I was his daughter. It was my place to help him. I gave up too soon."

"I refuse to let you blame yourself. You were only a young girl. There was no way you could have understood what was happening."

"I should have tried harder."

"It wouldn't have done any good."

She whirled around. "How do you know? How does anyone know? Maybe one more letter from me would have made the difference. That one extra letter might have given him the courage to mail one of these letters or cards."

A severe frown grooved lines across Burke's forehead. "How many years did you write him? Six, seven years? That's a long time for one so young and so sensitive to be continually rebuffed. You must realize that it wasn't your fault. You have to remember I saw your father during those years. We tried to help him, but no one could reach him. There's no point in tormenting yourself over this, Cara. Self-recriminations at this point are useless."

Her shoulders slumped. "I suppose you're right. Still, I'll never be quite sure about whether one more letter would have made the difference or not, will I?"

After what he'd been through at Shamrock, he couldn't tolerate even the few feet of office space separating them. He went to her. "Cara, I can't stand to see you unhappy. Dwell on the good that's come out of this. You know now that your father really did love you."

And maybe, he thought silently, pulling her into his arms, this new knowledge would restore a sense of balance to her and give them a chance for a real life together.

Seven

"Dammit, Burke! I should have known! There's no excuse for what happened!"

Cara was sitting in the corner of the study watching Cougar stride back and forth in front of Burke, who was sitting behind his desk. Cougar was an impressive sight, as his magnificent hair whipped about his shoulders and seemed almost to quiver with his anger. But in her opinion, he was no match for Burke.

An ominous rage smoldered beneath Burke's stillness. An elbow rested casually on the arm of his chair, but the hand of that arm was clenched into a fist. He was staring out the window, to all intents and purposes looking at the scenery. But Cara had seen those eyes before they had turned to the window, and she knew the green depths contained a dark wrath.

"Don't blame yourself. I underestimated the man too." His voice was low, quiet, but with an underlying vibration that gave his words an earsplitting intensity. "Davis lured me away from the security of Killara. You couldn't have foreseen his plan. No one could have."

"But I *should* have! When I think about York—"

Burke swung his chair around. "It wasn't serious, Cougar. And Rafe's loss was trivial."

"You have to let me call in the police."

"Absolutely not. We've handled things like this before, and we will this time too. I had more than my share of banner headlines during the trial. The last thing I want is even more of the blasted media swarming around us. They and the police would only complicate matters."

Cougar cursed under his breath. "Davis wants you bad, Burke, and he's cunning."

"Then pull out all the stops. Put every available resource at our command on this and then get more." Slowly Burke stood up and he leaned toward Cougar. His hands splayed flat on the desk, supporting his weight; the Delaney emerald showed prominently. "*That bastard used a gun against my family.*"

Cougar looked at Burke for a moment, nodded, then turned and left. Burke settled back in his chair and rested his forehead in the palm of his hand.

His distress drew Cara to his side. "Are you all right, Burke?" He didn't answer her, and she went down on her knees in front of him. "Burke?"

He raised his head. "I'm just so damn mad. York or Rafe could have been seriously hurt because of me."

"For heaven's sake! You worry about everyone

but yourself. You could have been *killed*, or hasn't that possibility even occurred to you?"

A small smile began to play around the corners of his mouth at her indignation on his behalf. "To tell you the truth, no. Now that I have you, I refuse to let anything happen to me."

Her brief spurt of anger died away and a tingling warmth took its place. "Now that you have me?" It wasn't so long ago that such possessive talk would have sent her running. Without analyzing the reasons, she moved closer. She lay her forearms along his thighs.

"I guess I shouldn't have said that." He rubbed his brow. "I don't really have you. Just because we're lovers, it doesn't mean you're mine, does it?"

Perhaps it was because of the emotional trauma he had gone through at Shamrock, Cara thought, but he had suddenly sounded so sad.

A surge of tenderness swept through her. "Come on. Why don't you go upstairs and take a shower? I'll go with you."

He smiled wearily. "Will you scrub my back?"

"Absolutely."

"Then you've got yourself a deal."

A particularly blue-skied morning graced the Sulphur Springs Valley as Bridget stooped to pull a perfectly formed head of lettuce from the rich soil. She shook it at Cara in satisfaction. "You won't find a sweeter-tasting lettuce anywhere on the face of this earth, now will you?"

"I'm certain you're right." Cara looked around her with gratitude. Here in Bridget's garden where quiet and harmony prevailed, she allowed herself to relax and offer unspoken thanks. The last few days had passed peacefully. There had been no more attempts on Burke's life, and there had been no more notes. And even though she had to consider the possibility that Burke was holding something back from her so that she wouldn't worry, he appeared very relaxed and happy. It seemed to her he even frowned less now.

Her gaze followed Bridget as she walked up and down the rows, fussing over the plants as if they were her babies. Cara had to smile. She herself had experienced Bridget's motherly care, and she had seen the way she positively doted on the Delaney brothers. Underneath Bridget's starchy primness was a woman with a maternal streak a mile long and with a lot of devotion to give.

"Bridget, forgive me if I'm asking a question that's out of line, but I'm curious about something. Why have you never married?"

Showing surprise but not resentment at Cara's question, the housekeeper straightened. "Well, now, I've always had responsibilities since I was but a girl. There was just never any time. Killara is not a house that runs smoothly on its own, is it?"

"You're very dedicated, and I'm sure the Delaneys have appreciated it, but haven't you ever wanted something more?"

"Faith! What's brought all these questions about?"

Cara shoved her hands into the back pockets of her jeans and looked down at the toe of one boot. She wasn't exactly sure of the answer to Bridget's question. The truth of the matter was she had felt unsettled ever since she read her father's letters. The letters had made her want to question the way she had chosen to live her life up to now, but she always stopped herself because she couldn't consider this problem without also examining her relationship with Burke and how she felt about him.

And added to her new knowledge of her father was the threat on Burke's life. She would have felt horror if she had heard *anyone's* life was in danger. But this wasn't anyone. This was Burke, and horror didn't begin to describe her feelings at the thought of something happening to him.

She had gone into an affair with him, thinking she was doing so on her terms and she would be able to handle it when it was over. Now she was very much afraid she had been fooling herself. She was no more in control of her feelings about their affair than she was in control of the sun. When she allowed herself to think about it, it scared her.

Since she didn't want to go into all of it with Bridget, she said, "I've been thinking about you and Cougar. It's obvious there's something between you."

"Ach! Isn't that the most ridiculous thing I've ever heard? I'm a home-loving woman, but a man like Cougar would never settle down. Cougar is a fitting name for that man! Why, you only have to look at him to see the wildness in him,"—her eyes cut uncertainly to Cara—"don't you now?"

"I admit that on the surface he appears a little unusual, but—"

"Unusual!" Bridget harrumphed. "I should say so! A person certainly tends to look twice at him, don't they? Why he's a fine figure of a man, isn't he? And his eyes, they remind me of black velvet, they're so soft and dark. And his hands! Have you ever noticed his hands, Cara?"

"Uh, no, I don't think I have."

"They're a man's hands. Strong. A woman would know she'd been held if those hands held her, yes she would." She nodded earnestly. "But then I've seen him pick up a wee baby bird that had fallen from its mother's nest, I have, and with hardly a flutter, that bird settled right into his hand. Knew it was safe, it did." Bridget's eyes had taken on a distant look. "He would be able to make a woman feel safe too."

Cara knelt and began picking at stray weeds, leaving Bridget alone with her thoughts, and she with hers. It was funny, but Bridget had just described how Cara felt about Burke. She had noticed that Bridget had become softer, younger-looking, since Cougar had been on the ranch. She wondered if becoming Burke's lover had wrought any changes in her that she was unaware of.

A forceful voice suddenly sliced through the peace of the afternoon. "You shouldn't have to be doing that! Doesn't Burke have people to take care of the weeding for you?"

Cara's head jerked around to see Cougar addressing Bridget, who had also taken to weeding several yards away. Both women stood up, but it was Bridget who held Cougar's attention.

"A little work in the good earth never hurt a soul, now did it?" Bridget asked indignantly, while her hand checked to make sure no stray curls had escaped from her French twist.

"I suppose that's true. But a woman like you shouldn't have to—"

"A woman like me, indeed! I suppose you're

referring to my age. You must think these bones of mine are too old for this sort of thing, now don't you? Well, I'll have you know—"

"As a matter of fact," Cougar cut in quietly, "I think your bones are fit for all sorts of activities. Would you like to hear about them?"

Bridget's color heightened. "N-no, of course, I wouldn't. Have you lost your mind?"

"I think I've just found it. The truth of the matter is, neither one of us is getting any younger, and we've wasted entirely too much time already."

"I'm sure I don't know what you're talking about."

"And another thing! Why don't you ever wear your hair down? You've got glorious hair, woman!"

Cara didn't wait to hear Bridget's retort. She slipped away, sure that she wouldn't be missed.

That evening Cougar and Bridget were nowhere to be found. Cara and Burke had dinner alone, undisturbed. Afterward they took a walk. Hand in hand they wandered across the lushly landscaped grounds immediately surrounding the house.

Burke felt like a man both blessed and torn. It wasn't easy to be so in love with a woman that he couldn't stand to be away from her for even a minute, and at the same time, being in the position of having to give her time and space to come to love him too. And what if she didn't? He pushed the thought away; it was intolerable.

She had kicked off her shoes and was walking beside him, barefoot, humming a little tune under her breath. He hoped she was as happy and carefree as she seemed. Since they had become lovers, long hours spent with her had taught him much about her. In some respects he had never known a woman as open and as honest as Cara. Yet she still kept portions of herself out of reach. She was too practiced at pulling away quickly.

Quicksilver.

And the quintessential woman.

A combination that had succeeded in knocking him for a loop.

At first glance the dress Cara was wearing tonight was simple—a shirtwaist with a full bodice and a circular skirt. Yet it was made of golden silk, and the wide skirt lay over champagne lace petticoats. He could hear the two fabrics murmuring and whispering as they strolled through the night. The sound enticed him.

"I have some good news."

"Oh? Tell me," Cara urged.

"Cougar has uncovered a lead on Davis. He thinks that it's only a matter of time until they have him."

"I hope so. I can't stand the thought that some maniac is out there trying to kill you."

"The thought doesn't exactly make my day either," Burke said lightly, "but I have to face the fact that I have enemies. As long as they don't attack my family or the people I love, though, I can handle it."

"How did you ever get a reputation for being hard and ruthless?" she asked in amazement.

"It's deserved, believe me." A harshness roughened his words. "I *will* protect what is mine with all the power at my command."

There was that possessiveness. She chose to

ignore it once again. "You are one of the most decent, caring men I've ever met in my life."

He laughed, pleased with her reaction. "I'm glad you think so. Maybe I should hire you as my PR person. What do you think?"

"That sounds like a full-time job. I'm not sure I'd be up to it."

Burke cursed silently. She thought he was trying to tie her down. That she was right only made him realize he should tread more carefully. He squeezed her hand. "Think about it." He stopped and turned to her. "I have a board meeting coming up in Tucson soon. Saturday to be precise."

Cara's heart sank. That meant he would be leaving her again, and she hated the idea. But then, she told herself in the next instant, she shouldn't. After all, there were no ties between the two of them, and she was being incredibly selfish, considering the two times he had had to leave the ranch had both been emergencies involving his brothers. "How long will you be gone?"

"From Killara? I don't know. Several days. From you? I was hoping no time at all. I'd like you to go with me. Remember? I mentioned it to you a couple of weeks ago. Did you forget?"

"I guess I did."

"Will you come with me? I have some work to do and I thought you might enjoy a change of scene."

An illogical pulse of happiness spurted through her. "Yes, I'd like that."

He nodded. "Good. Rafe and York will be coming in on Saturday. I know they'd enjoy seeing you again after all these years."

"I don't know about that," she said doubtfully. "Though at any rate I'd really love to see them."

Nervously her tongue licked her bottom lip. "How do you think they'll feel about me and you? You know—"

"They'll be delighted," he finished for her, and raised her hand to his mouth for a tender kiss. "I thought we could fly into Tucson a day or two early. That way I could get some business done while you shopped or saw a few movies or whatever."

"You don't have to worry about entertaining me, you know. You make whatever plans you need to, and I'll adapt."

His fingers brushed her cheek lightly. "I guess I worry that you'll get bored."

"Get bored with you?" Cara asked, genuinely incredulous. "Why on earth would you think that?"

"You're used to a jet-set type of life."

That a self-assured man like Burke Delaney would feel even a particle of uncertainty because of her made her feel very humble. "You listen to me," she said solemnly. "I've seen the Seven Wonders of the World, but none of them have ever taken my breath away like you can. With just a look you can make me feel an exhilaration like nothing or no one ever has. If there's a fear of boredom between us, then it's that you will become tired of me."

He had become very still, totally riveted by her words. "Then we have no problem at all, do we?" he asked softly.

Suddenly Cara broke free of Burke. With her laughter ringing through the night she did a spectacular series of cartwheels right across the lawn, finally collapsing amid a froth of silk and lace.

Captivated by her unpredictability and exuberance, Burke came down beside her. "I don't believe

I've ever had anyone do cartwheels across my lawn at midnight!"

"How extremely dull for you!"

His hand covered her rapidly beating heart. "Are you as happy as you seem?"

"Oh, yes. Very."

He buried his face in the soft skin at her neck. "It's going to last," he promised.

She shivered as she felt his breath against her skin. "Make love to me, Burke."

He drew back. "Here? Now?"

"Yes." Her arms went around his neck. "I want you now!"

His blood began to pound. Cara was a fantasy that had come to him, making his life more real and filling it completely. Her hair spread around her head on the dark green grass, silver as spun moonlight. Her wild sweet scent whirled around him.

He crushed his mouth to hers, and she responded with a sudden desperation. As always, the raw passion that flamed so easily between them surprised him, but it shouldn't have. At times like this he was sure that Cara had invented lovemaking. No woman had ever been so uninhibited with him, so wild. No woman had ever been able to take him so high and satisfy him so completely.

Urgently his fingers sought her buttons until he had laid open the golden silk material and exposed the pale gold skin of her breasts. By the light of the moon her perfectly formed breasts were a sight to be worshiped, but the fast-rising heat building inside his body wouldn't allow it. The fire within him demanded that his fingers cup the firm mounds, that his teeth gently pull at the rigid crests. He did, and she arched to him, making demands of her own.

His hands went to her legs and beneath her dress he found no stockings, only bare silken flesh. A moan wrenched from her throat, and her hands joined his and slowly began to strip off her panties.

Need drove him to capture, to have, to hold. There was no time to remove all their clothes, only the necessary items. He unzipped his trousers, and she reached for him. When her hand touched him, then closed around him, a fire flashed to the center of his stomach with the impact of an exploding bullet.

She rolled on top of him, fitting them together, and the night closed in around them. No words were needed. Their bodies were in control. Their hands touched aggressively; their mouths ravaged.

He held back, allowing her the freedom to move as her desires demanded. Her small palms pressed flat against his chest as her hips rotated urgently. His jaw clenched with the effort required of him, but the pain of his restraint was of the most exquisite type.

From beneath his half-lowered lids he saw her above him. Her breasts gently swayed inside the gaped bodice of her dress, and her nipples were harder than he had ever seen them. Her head was thrown back, her lips were parted, and a deep sweet moan came from her throat.

It was all too much. He pulled her down to him, and she poured herself over him, liquid and hot as starlight, driving him to madness . . . and then beyond.

Eight

"Now, I hate to admit it, but I wager Killara will do very well without me indeed!" Bridget nodded her head emphatically and adjusted her apron. Her red hair spilled in a series of ripples down her back, completely free of any restraining pins. "Why I'm sure Esther Copeland can do just as good as I." She paused in midnod and her brow knitted doubtfully. "Well . . . perhaps not *quite* as good, but a reasonable enough job, I'm sure, aren't I?"

"Are you?" Cara's uncertain tone revealed her difficulty in adjusting to Bridget's sudden decision to leave Killara and make a new life with Cougar. "Bridget, I knew there were feelings between you and Cougar, but—this! You're talking about throwing over your whole way of life."

Bridget refilled Cara's coffee cup, then her own. "I suppose I am, aren't I?"

"It—it just seems so drastic!" Cara tried to calm herself down and to analyze as objectively as possible her shock at Bridget's decision. After all, it was really none of her business. Still, Cougar and Bridget's marriage plans seemed to probe at something sensitive inside her, and she couldn't say why. "Bridget, you made your decision literally overnight. Don't you think you should take a little more time and think about it?"

Bridget blushed at the reference to overnight, but remained resolute. "Cara, lass, listen to me. It's not as sudden as you think. Cougar and I have known each other for a while, but we were two people who had lived single our whole lives and were set in our ways, now weren't we? And we were each of us afraid to be the one to speak first."

"So what happened? What was the one thing that made you know he was right for you?"

Bridget shrugged her broad shoulders. "Who's to say? You can't analyze these things too much, lass, or you'll go crazy. Maybe the sun was in the right spot yesterday afternoon when he came to the garden. Maybe the moon was the right fullness last night when—" She turned her head away to pat her French twist, but instead found her hair loose. "Well, never mind. That's not important, is it now?"

Cara took a sip of her coffee. "I'm sorry, Bridget. I shouldn't be interfering. It's just that some things have been bothering me lately, that's all. A lot has happened to me since I've been on Killara."

Bridget cast her a shrewd glance. "And you're trying to make some decisions of your own, now aren't you?"

"I thought I had already made them," Cara said dryly.

"Ach! But then life is never tidy, is it?"

"No, I suppose not, but"—a heavy sigh escaped from her—"it would be a lot easier if it were."

"Easier, yes, but perhaps not as exciting."

Cara's eyebrows rose with surprise at Bridget's statement. The older woman hadn't made it a question.

"I know what you're thinking, don't I? That Cougar and I are two very different people, and that what I'm about to do is a gamble."

"Well, yes, I guess that is what I'm thinking."

"I've had a good life on Killara. Up until yesterday I had fully expected—and even looked forward—to ending my days here. But I've gone my whole life without someone of my very own to love and to love me back, haven't I?" She nodded her head emphatically. "Then Cougar came along. Now, he's a man who strikes one as half wild, doesn't he though? But you know what he told me yesterday?"

Cara shook her head. "What?"

"He has a small ranch, all his very own, in a beautiful little valley in the upper part of the state. Using every spare moment he's had these past few years, he's built it up, and now he says it's ready to be a home and not just a ranch. Can you imagine that?"

"That is wonderful, Bridget."

"This is my chance, Cara, and I'm going to take it. I don't want to get to the end of my life and have nothing but regrets for a love I wasn't brave enough to reach out for, now do I?"

Cara remained quiet.

Smiling kindly, Bridget patted Cara's hand. "You'll figure it out, won't you, lass? I know you will." She stood and bustled off, leaving Cara to ponder their conversation.

She had never thought of herself as a coward, merely as practical. But in the last few weeks she had come back to Killara, met Burke and become his lover, found the letters her father had never had the courage to mail to her, and seen two very different people, Cougar and Bridget, come together. Too much change, too fast, had left Cara with too many questions. She felt as though her head were spinning.

Burke's work in Tucson didn't leave much time for him and Cara to be together. Even though she missed him, she understood. And it gave her a chance to get back to a part of her own life that was very dear to her.

On Friday morning, the day before York and Rafe were to fly in, Cara tiptoed into Burke's office.

Located in one large corner of Delaney Tower on the nineteenth floor, the office was decorated in Southwestern decor, as was his penthouse apartment one floor above. Both were done in colors of the desert and mountains—sand, taupe, rose, and mauve. The sofas and chairs were plush and rounded, with no harsh angles. Plants and cactus abounded among well-lighted pieces of art, many of which seemed sculptured by nature. The office was contemporary and sophisticated, with a touch of the primitive, she thought, like the man sitting behind the desk.

Cara smiled as she approached the massive desk that was set at an angle against two walls of windows. Burke was deep in thought as he studied some papers in front of him. "Am I disturbing you?"

Looking up, he saw her, and his frown of concentration disappeared. "Not at all! I thought you'd sleep much later, so I deliberately didn't wake you."

"I can't imagine why you thought I would need extra sleep."

He laughed. "It couldn't be, could it, that you burn the candle at both ends?"

"You seem to be awake all the hours I am." She flashed him a saucy grin and perched on the side of the desk. The calf-length white lace skirt she had put on this morning fanned from her thigh to the floor in an exotic semicircle. Her freshly brushed silver-blond hair flowed over the shoulders of an oversize cream-colored cotton knit sweater. A beige leather belt lay flat across her stomach, and one beige-booted foot rested on the floor, while the other, inches off the floor, swung back and forth.

Burke pushed back from his desk, got up, and went to her. "That's because I'm afraid I might miss something."

"Ah, well, I suppose that explains it."

He pulled her off the desk and into his arms. "Explains what?"

"Anything you want it to."

He bent his head and kissed her, and she responded to him as though she had been doing it all her life.

"How come," he asked with a husky catch in his throat, "you look so beautiful in the morning?" His mouth went to the side of her neck. "And at noon?" His lips traveled to the hollow at the center of her throat. "And at night?"

She swayed into him. "I don't know."

His mouth found the perfumed pulse point behind her ear and began nibbling. "It was very hard for me to concentrate on business this morning, when I could picture you just one floor above me, still in bed, all golden and soft and sweet."

She gave a little laugh. "So why didn't you come and wake me up?"

"That's a good question. What do you have on underneath this sweater?"

"That's also a good question. Why don't you find out?"

"Because if I did, I wouldn't stop there." He reluctantly pulled away. "Do you have to be so uninhibited?"

"I thought men liked their women to be uninhibited."

"Only when they don't have work to do. I have a board meeting to preside over in the morning, and believe me, it's hard enough to get my brothers into town for a business meeting as it is. I have to have everything ready for them."

She smiled. "Oh, well, since you've explained it so charmingly, then okay, I'll leave."

"Not so fast." He hated letting her go. He drew her back to him for another quick hungry kiss. "What are you going to do today?"

She danced out of his arms. "Lots of things!"

"Should I be jealous?" He had intended to ask the question teasingly, but somehow it had come out menacingly.

She burst out laughing. "Absolutely!"

"Well, will you at least come back and have lunch with me?" he asked on a plaintive note.

She was already at the door before she turned and waved. "I'm sorry. I don't think I can. Bye."

Burke stared at the closed door for a minute,

smiling a bit ruefully. Then he shook his head and went back to work.

By late afternoon Burke's indulgent good humor had vanished. Cara had never been away from him for a whole day before, and he had missed her like hell. He wanted her back with him. Now. Where could she be anyway? His phone rang and he reached for it. "Hello?"

A female voice asked, "May I speak to Miss Winston please? Miss Cara Winston."

Burke frowned at the phone. To his knowledge Cara had received no phone calls and no mail since she had been in Arizona. "She's not here at the moment. May I ask who's calling?"

"This is Dr. Cooper's office at Tucson Medical Center. Could you ask her to call us as soon as you can?"

"May I ask what this is in reference to?"

"Just tell her that it concerns the test results she was anxious to hear about. Thank you."

The line went dead. Burke slowly lowered the receiver, and a knot began tightening in his stomach.

Why was a doctor's office calling Cara? Was she sick? No, no. He dismissed the idea. He would certainly know it if she had been ill. A picture of her as she had been this morning rose in his mind. She had been radiant and vital, gaily waving good-bye to him and skipping out the door.

He got up from his desk and strode to the window. The view from his windows encompassed miles, but he saw none of it. Instead his mind was racing busily. The woman had mentioned test results. *What* test results?

All of a sudden a pain pierced his heart so fiercely that his hand actually went to his chest. My God! Could she be pregnant?

He tried to think. It was true that they had been lovers for only two weeks, but it seemed to him that he had heard somewhere that there was a blood test that could detect pregnancy within seventy-two hours of conception.

Had something happened to make her believe she might be pregnant? Fool! he cursed himself. Why *wouldn't* she think she was pregnant? She hadn't been on the Pill when they had started making love. She had been a virgin, for God's sake! And they had been isolated on the ranch for most of the time since. There had been no opportunity for her to see a doctor about contraception.

He, on the other hand, had thought to use protection, but only after that first night. And, he reminded himself grimly, there were a few other times, like the night when they had made love on the lawn, when his desire for her had swept him away and using a contraceptive had dropped to the very bottom on his list of priorities.

He had been so singleminded about his love for her and his hope that she would come to love him, he had forgotten all about the possibility of Cara's becoming pregnant.

Suddenly he grew still, and his spine turned to ice. Was that really the truth? His hands gripped the back of his leather chair. Maybe it wasn't. Maybe the truth was he *hadn't* overlooked the possibility. After all, before Cara had come into his life, he had always gone to great lengths to make sure that the women he slept with would not become pregnant. He had fallen passionately in love with Cara, but he hadn't lost all his reason.

Maybe deep down something had told him that the only way he was ever going to hold Cara was to get her pregnant. He didn't like to think he would do that, but it was making more and more sense to him. Why else would he have neglected to be more careful?

Damn! He picked up a marble paperweight and threw it across the room. It hit the opposite wall with a crash that brought both his secretary and a security guard running in.

He took a deep, steadying breath and held up his hand. "I'm all right." To his secretary he said, "I'm going up to the apartment, but I don't want to be disturbed unless it's an emergency."

With her arms filled with packages Cara opened the door of the apartment and entered the darkened living room. "Burke," she called. "Burke, are you here?"

He reached over and switched on the light beside his chair.

"Oh, good, you *are* here. I was afraid you'd still be in the office. Wait until you see what I've bought!" She tossed her packages onto a sofa, but retained one.

"Where have you been?"

"Can't you tell?" she asked with a teasing lilt to her voice. "I found some of the greatest shops in the Foothills Mall. I'm sure the sales personnel there will be talking about my shopping trip for years to come." She pulled out a diaphanous bit of lingerie and looked at it perplexed. "No, that's not it." She flung it aside and reached for another bag.

"That's not what?" he asked, barely able to restrain his impatience. There was so much he needed to find out from her. The wait for her return had seemed interminable.

"What I want to show you." She glanced at the lace blouse in her hand, then tossed it on a chair. "That's not it either."

"It can wait, Cara."

"But it's for you!" She delved into another bag. "I bought you a shirt. The stripe on it is the *exact* color of your eyes, and I can't wait to see it on you."

"Later!"

She had never heard him raise his voice, and it brought her head around with a snap. "Good heavens, Burke! What's wrong?"

"Where have you been?"

She stared at him in bewilderment. "I told you. I've been shopping. I'm sorry if I'm late, but I deliberately stayed away all day so that you could get some work done."

"Where else did you go?"

She shrugged. "No place special."

"Cara!" Her name was shouted with such suppressed violence that she actually took a step away from him. "Why don't you want me to know that you were at the hospital today?"

"The hospital." She paled. "How did you find out?"

"Someone from Dr. Cooper's office called and left a message for you."

"What was the message?"

"For you to call." His words were bitten out. "It

seems the test results you were so anxious about
are in."

"I see." She sat down and eyed him speculatively.

"I want an explanation, Cara."

"About what?"

"Dammit! Don't do this to me! To us."

"I'm afraid I don't know why you're so upset,
Burke. You've obviously gotten the wrong idea
about something, but for the life of me I can't figure out what it is."

"Are you pregnant?"

The question hit her like a blow. "Pregnant! Is
that what all this is about? You're afraid that I'm
pregnant?"

"Are you?"

"How should I know?" She jumped up and
strode angrily to the other side of the room.

"Then why did you go to the hospital today?"

She whirled toward him. "That is *my* business
and no one else's."

"Cara"—he raked his hand through his hair—
"you don't understand. I was so afraid—"

"Afraid? Afraid that I was trying to trap the great
Burke Delaney with a baby? Now that I think about
it, I'm surprised you haven't had me sign some sort
of paper, stating that no matter how many times
we have made love or will make love, you will not be
responsible for any offspring."

He grabbed her by the arms. "I would gladly and
willingly take the responsibility for any baby of
mine. The question is, would you do the same?"

It felt as though his words had sliced into her
flesh. Her voice faltered. "What kind of question is
that?"

"A reasonable one!"

"There's not one damn thing reasonable about any part of this conversation, Burke!"

He suddenly became aware of how tightly his fingers were pressing into the flesh of her upper arms. He released her. "I'm sorry. Did I hurt you?"

"No." His grip hadn't hurt, but she rubbed her arm anyway. A reflex. "I think you owe me an explanation, Burke."

"You're right." He ran his hand around the back of his neck. "Sit down." She hesitated. "Please?" She complied. "You deserve to hear this, and maybe after you do, you'll understand a little bit better why I was"—he shrugged—"afraid. There's no other word for what I've been feeling this afternoon." His jaw clenched as he pulled his thoughts together. "Have you ever heard anyone mention a girl named Elise?"

"Yes, Bridget mentioned her name once."

He nodded. "We met when we were in college. I was twenty and she was nineteen. We were very young, and as it turned out, very foolish."

Now that she had calmed down, she could hear the pain in his voice, and she recognized that, right from the start, that same pain had been underneath his anger and his accusations. "Why do you say that?"

"Elise became pregnant. I was ecstatic and she told me she was too. I wanted to make immediate plans to be married, but she kept stalling, making excuses. What I didn't know was that she was making plans of her own, plans she couldn't face me with. She had decided she couldn't handle the responsibility of a baby—or of marriage to me. One weekend, without telling me, she and one of her girlfriends drove across the border to Nogales.

Back then Nogales had *brujas*—witches—who ran thriving, if unsanitary, abortion clinics."

"Oh, no!"

He flashed her a mirthless grin. "If only she had trusted me enough to tell me what was going through her mind, I would have done everything in my power to talk her out of it, but in the end I would have helped her. It would have killed me, but somehow, some way, I would have found her someone safe to perform the abortion, even if I had had to fly an American doctor into Mexico to do it. Or at least I would like to think I would have. One thing is for certain, I would never have allowed her to go to a *bruja*." He shrugged. "Maybe she didn't love me after all. I don't know. But I'll never forget that weekend. Her girlfriend called from Nogales, hysterical."

Cara remained silent, knowing there was more to come and knowing he had to tell her.

"I arrived in time for Elise to die in my arms. The accusing look on her face will haunt me forever."

"But it shouldn't! What she did wasn't your fault."

He shrugged.

Suddenly she gasped. "Is that what you were afraid of? That if I found out I was pregnant, I might abort the baby? You don't just jump to conclusions, do you, Burke? You take a flying leap!"

"Cara, you've created a life-style that enables you to remain free from any sort of entanglements."

Her eyebrows drew together in bewilderment. "Any sort of— The *baby*! You thought I would get rid of a baby growing inside of me because it might tie me down?"

"Cara." He reached for her, but she drew back.

"Don't touch me!"

He winced at the impact of her cry. "I'm sorry." He swiveled away and thrust his hands in his pockets. "I had no right to accuse you. No matter what has happened in my past, I shouldn't have accused you." His voice was quiet, and his broad shoulders slumped.

Cara's throat tightened with pain, but she wasn't sure if it was because of his pain or hers. Certainly his experience with Elise, and then most recently, the paternity suit, made it understandable that he would be sensitive about the possibility of a woman being pregnant with his baby. And she certainly qualified in that category, she thought without humor. Then Dr. Cooper's office had called and left a message for her concerning test results. The idea of what he must have gone through since the call gradually defused her anger.

"Burke?" He slowly turned toward her, his body stiff, every muscle drawn taut. "It's all right," she said softly, but firmly.

"No, it isn't. It was a dumb, stupid thing for me to do, flying off the handle like that, jumping to the conclusion that you were pregnant. I have only one excuse."

"I know. Elise, and then with the paternity suit, the issue of a woman being pregnant with your baby was fresh in your mind."

"No. That's not it."

"Then what?"

"I love you, Cara, almost to the point of madness, and you might as well know it."

She stared at him, not sure she had heard right.

His mouth twisted into a crooked grin. "You didn't expect that, did you?"

She felt as if the floor had just been snatched from under her. "N-no."

"Love is always unexpected," he said gently. "I'm hoping you'll find out soon."

Her hand swept through her hair in agitation, and she could feel herself tensing. It had been her experience that with love came hurt.

Perhaps Burke could see her thoughts mirrored in her eyes, because he said, "We're not going to have any big discussion about this tonight. I don't want to frighten you, and I'm going to give you plenty of time to accept the idea. But, Cara, I want you to know that my love is not going to change. It's something you'll be able to count on your whole life. All you have to do is reach out and take it."

Cara looked down at her hands and discovered them clasped tightly together. She forced herself to relax them. "I'd like to tell you what I was doing at the hospital today," she said slowly.

"You don't have to. You were right. It's none of my business."

"No, I want you to know. Come sit down with me." She waited until they both had sat down. "I've already told you that my various stepfathers bestowed an awful lot of money on me. An obscene amount really, especially when you consider I did nothing to earn it. At any rate, early on I decided I wanted to do something special with it, something other than just donate to medical research, which I do on a routine basis. So I had my lawyers in London set up a trust to fulfill critically and terminally ill children's wishes.

"Wherever I go around the world, I have my lawyers contact the local hospital and find one or two children for whom my money could make a difference in their last days. Then once the lawyers have provided the hospital with my credentials, I go and visit the children. I talk with them and find out what they would like most in the world." A soft smile curved her lips. "I love talking to them. Most of their cases are hopeless, but they're so brave. I always come away feeling quite inadequate.

"Today I met a little girl who a year ago was diagnosed as having leukemia. They never expected her to live this long, but she's fooled them all. She wants more than anything to go to Disneyland, and I'm going to see that she gets there. We were waiting for the results of her latest tests before making final plans though. Those were the test results the doctor's nurse mentioned to you."

"You make me feel very ashamed."

"Don't be." She reached over and took his hand. "I told you, it's all right. And we've both learned some things about each other tonight."

"I love you, even more than I did a few minutes ago, and I didn't think that was possible."

She looked down at their joined hands, then back up at him. "Take me to bed and hold me."

"I can't think of anything I want to do more."

She awoke at dawn. They hadn't drawn the curtains the night before, and now the first rays of the rising sun were making their way into the room through the immense windows. She was curled against the warmth and solidity of Burke's body. Carefully, so that she wouldn't wake him, she shifted away from him and raised up on one elbow so that she could get a better look at him.

She remembered that Bridget had told her

Burke had had to be strong. Well, he was—and so much more. A great man knew how to use his strength. She had learned that Burke did. He was a hard man, it was true, but there was also a gentleness in him. He lavished it on her. And there was loyalty and compassion—qualities to be admired and respected.

In the gradually brightening light she could see his black lashes lying heavily against the bronzed skin of his cheek. Even in sleep he didn't look vulnerable, but she knew he was. He had been almost out of his mind with worry last night when he believed she might be pregnant.

A sudden thought occurred to her. A baby. She couldn't think of anything more marvelous. A tiny person who would be part her, part Burke, but all itself. No baby could have a better father. He would be loving and protective.

She was pretty sure she wasn't pregnant, however, and today she would go to the doctor to insure that there would be no surprises for them along those lines. But still. A baby! A perfect symbol of their love. . . . Their love.

Oh, God, it had happened! She loved him, and the depth of her love for him threatened to swamp her.

She lowered her head to the pillow beside Burke and turned her face toward his. For long moments her body trembled with the shock, but as she slowly absorbed the knowledge the trembling stopped and the wonder of her love took over.

Burke had said she would be able to count on his love her whole life, and she believed him. She could walk into his arms and never be afraid that he'd let her go. He would hold her for all time.

She suppressed the urge to wake him and tell him. She didn't want him groggy with sleep. She wanted the moment to be as special as she could make it. Perhaps she would ask the cook to prepare a champagne breakfast.

In his sleep Burke reached for her, and she nestled closer, feeling a certain and warm peace. Her newly discovered serenity sank in all the way to her bones, and she slept.

Nine

Cara awoke with the feeling that something important had happened. Then it came to her like a flash. She loved Burke. Immediately she reached out for him, but he was gone.

Of course! His meeting was this morning, and his brothers were due in. They were probably already here! Quickly thrusting back the covers, she jumped out of bed.

Thirty minutes later, showered and dressed, she went directly to the kitchen. Burke was at the table, drinking coffee, and with him were Rafe and York Delaney.

The three Delaney brothers—the Shamrock Trinity. They were legends, and Cara could easily see why. Together their individual power became magnified, and they sent out the loud, clear message of utter invincibility.

Although she hadn't seen York and Rafe since she was a little girl, certain things remained true of both of them, and she had no trouble deciding which brother was which.

York, with his dark features and vivid blue eyes, had retained the beauty of his youth, but with the years had come a maturity that had complemented the perfection of his features, making him the most beautiful man she had ever seen in her life. Not handsome. *Beautiful.* Added to that was a brooding air that only increased his astonishing effect on a person.

Rafe on the other hand had good looks that were more unconventional. He had the same bronze-dark skin and black hair as his brothers, but when he laughed—as he was doing now in reference to something Burke had said—his looks turned roguish and his black eyes positively danced.

Her gaze went to Burke, and her heart swelled with love. She couldn't deny that his features showed a harshness and a ruthlessness that had escaped Rafe and York. But it didn't bother her. She knew how gentle and understanding he could be. He had told her that he loved her, without asking her for any commitment in return. He had allowed her to see inside of him and exposed areas of himself to her that were painful.

He was the man she loved with all her heart, and she was sorry now that she hadn't given into her earlier urge to wake him and tell him of her love.

She saw Burke turn to York. "I gather you haven't worked out your problem yet."

York shrugged, and the jacket of his custom-made suit stretched over his broad shoulders. "There are some problems that don't have any solutions."

"Maybe not, but problems are sometimes a hell of a lot easier to bear if they're shared."

"I appreciate it, but it's nothing you and Rafe can help me with."

"Not unless you let us," Rafe said.

"Look, if it was anything else . . ." He stirred uneasily in his chair, then said decisively, "No, I have to deal with it myself."

"All right, we won't push," Burke said. "But you know we're here."

York smiled. "Haven't you always been?"

"Yes," Rafe said, and grinned. "It's just that you weren't always smart enough to know it."

York's eyes narrowed on his younger brother. "Why don't we talk about something else for a while? Like . . . your positively *splendiferous* appearance."

Rafe pretended outrage. "Splendiferous! I'll have you know—"

"Cara!" Burke had just seen her. He stood and crossed the room to her. "Good morning. How long have you been up?"

"Not long. I woke at dawn, but then fell asleep again. The next thing I knew, it was nine o'clock."

"I'm glad you got some extra sleep." He pulled her into his arms and, regardless of his brothers' presence, kissed her with tender passion. By the time he released her, she was shaking.

Taking her hand, he led her to the table and his two brothers rose.

"Oh, please," she protested, extremely nervous at meeting them, "don't get up on my account."

Their only response was to smile charmingly at her, worsening her state of nerves. After all, these

men were the two most important people in the
world to Burke.

"Rafe and York, I'd like you to meet—"

"You don't have to tell us who this is," Rafe said,
stepping forward and taking her hand away from
Burke. "This is the merger you've been working so
hard on." He dropped a gallant kiss on the back of
her hand, and when he raised his head from her
hand, Cara could see that his black eyes were glit-
tering merrily.

"Merger?" she asked.

"We've been worried about Burke," York said,
taking her hand away from Rafe, and holding it
with a real warmth. "He told us that he's been
working extra hard lately on a merger, but he
wouldn't let us in on any of the details. Now we
understand why. Hello. By the way, I'm York."

"I know," she said, breathing deeply, trying to
pull air into her lungs. These Delaneys had a way of
taking your breath away.

Rafe's winged brows shot up. "You know him
and not me! That's not fair!"

"Sibling rivalry is really a terrible thing," Burke
remarked to her, leading her to the table and
pulling out a chair for her. "I have such a time with
these two."

Cara laughed. "I don't believe a word of it. And
Rafe, I know you too. I remember teaching you how
to play jacks."

York's blue eyes cut to Burke. "Isn't that interesting? I never knew Rafe played jacks."

"I never did," Rafe denied flatly.

"Yes, you did," Cara said, as the brothers settled
back into their chairs around the table. "One sum-
mer afternoon you happened to be riding by the

foreman's house on Killara and saw a lonely little girl playing by herself on the porch. You stopped to talk to me and—"

"Cara Winston! You're Bill Winston's daughter!"

"That's right."

"Well, I'll be damned."

"That's right," Burke agreed. "Cara, would you like some coffee?"

"Please."

"How long have you been back?" York asked.

"About a month. It's been wonderful being on Killara again."

"How long are you going to stay?"

Since she wanted to tell Burke of her love for him in private, she wasn't sure how to answer York. But Burke saved her from having to answer by cutting in smoothly. "I think that's one of those things we're still negotiating. Now, you two behave. I don't want Cara embarrassed."

Rafe looked shocked. "*Us* embarrass someone with probing, tactless questions? Heaven forbid!"

York took the clue from his older brother. "Speaking of someone embarrassing himself, Rafe was preparing to tell us about his suit when you came in, Cara."

"My suit can't be embarrassing *and* splendiferous," Rafe maintained. "Make up your mind."

"We think your suit is"—Burke took his time in searching for just the right word—"*white.*"

Rafe brushed an imaginary speck of lint from the sleeve of his jacket. "It's obvious to me that you're both eaten up with jealousy over my suit, and I think it's time I had a woman's opinion. Cara?"

Hardly able to contain her laughter, she said,

"Oh, I definitely like it, and the whole outfit is beautifully coordinated."

"You can say that again," York muttered. "Everything—his jacket, his pants, his shirt, his tie, his handkerchief, his shoes, his socks—*everything* is white!"

"Is there some special occasion to warrant all this finery?" Burke asked. "Something other than the board meeting, I mean."

"Honestly! If you two keep this up, you'll give Cara the impression that I don't normally dress well, when in fact the exact opposite is true. Why, I often wear this very suit to muck out the stables."

Hoots of laughter erupted from everyone.

"It must be hell on those shoes," York offered.

"Actually the substance that I quite often find myself stepping in conditions the leather."

"Conditions the leather!" York repeated.

"Not many people know that."

Burke glanced at his watch. "I'm sorry to break this up, gentlemen, but we do have a meeting and we have quite a bit of business to cover."

Rafe and York groaned. Burke looked at Cara. "You'd think I was inviting them to their own hanging rather than a meeting to tell them that they're richer than they were the last quarter."

Smiling, she rose from the table. "I need to get going too. Rafe and York, it was nice seeing you again."

"It sure was." Rafe grinned. "I'll even forgive you for spilling the beans about my playing jacks."

"I'm sure we'll see you again soon," York said.

"What are you planning to do today?" Burke asked, drawing her a short distance away from his brothers.

"I'm going to do a little shopping for some of the kids I met at the hospital yesterday. I thought maybe some stuffed animals might be welcome."

"I bet they will be." He reached into his pocket and drew out six one-hundred-dollar bills.

"Burke, you don't have to give me money. I have my own."

"I know, but the work you do for the kids at the hospital is important to you, and I'd like to be a part of it in a small way."

She took the money from him and reached up to kiss his lips gently. "Thank you. That means a lot to me. Your money will go for the softest, most huggable stuffed animals I can find." She paused. "Listen, are Rafe and York going to be here for dinner tonight?"

"Rafe is heading back to Shamrock as soon as the meeting is over. I'm not sure about York. Why?"

She chewed on her bottom lip. "Well, I was wondering if we could have dinner alone, but if York is staying over . . ."

"If you want to have dinner alone, then we will, but—" He frowned. "Is something wrong? Didn't you like York and Rafe?"

"I like them very much," she assured him with complete sincerity. "They're wonderful, but then how could they be anything else? They're your brothers."

"Then what—"

"Nothing, nothing at all. Just an odd fancy of mine." She smiled up at him. "Okay?" He nodded, but he was still frowning. Lightly she ran a finger across the deeply etched lines of his forehead. "I'm going to cure you of that habit yet. I'll see you this afternoon."

A few hours later Cara was sitting on the floor of a toy store, literally waist-deep in stuffed animals. She had bought them all, and a lot more, and was waiting for the sales clerk to hand her the final bill. If the store couldn't deliver her purchases to the hospital this afternoon, she had decided she would hire a fleet of taxis and do the job herself.

"Miss Winston?"

"Yes." She glanced up. The man who had addressed her was a stranger, but the worried expression he wore caught her attention, even as she noticed he was conservatively dressed in a three-piece dark brown suit. Somehow she didn't think he was associated with the toy store. "Is something wrong?"

"I'm afraid you're going to have to come with me."

For a man he had an abnormally high-pitched voice, she thought, and her brows drew together in puzzlement. "I beg your pardon?"

"I'm Carl Robbins with the Cougar Jones Security Agency." He pulled out an identification card and offered it for her inspection. "Something's happened to Mr. Delaney, and they've sent me for you."

Instantly she came to her feet. "Oh, my God! What's happened? Is he all right?"

"I'll explain on the way. Mr. Delaney is asking for you, and I'm afraid we have very little time."

* * *

Burke looked down the table. "Am I boring you, Rafe?"

"What?" Rafe looked at his oldest brother blankly, then as he realized what was going on, a sheepish grin began to spread over his face.

"You're a million miles away from here."

"Maybe not so far," York remarked quietly. "Maybe his thoughts are only as far as Shamrock."

Burke raised an eyebrow at the secretary taking notes. "Could you bring us some coffee, please?" He waited until she had left the room, then leaned back in his chair. "I didn't want to bring it up before now, but you're positively glowing. What's made you so happy?"

Rafe cleared his throat and pointed to the papers in front of him. "Sure, I'm happy. As you can see, Shamrock has had an excellent quarter."

"Those are the figures for Hell's Bluff," York said.

"Oh." Rafe's eyes quickly scanned the column of figures in question. "Well, I'm *also* very happy about how well Hell's Bluff is doing."

Burke and York exchanged amused glances, and Rafe gave up. "I'm that obvious, huh?" Rafe asked.

"Painfully," Burke said dryly. "Come on, brother, let us in on it."

Just then the door opened and the secretary hurried in, her face white. "Mr. Delaney, there's a call for you on line one. It's that Mr. Davis, and he says it's an emergency."

"Davis!" York exclaimed.

"Get Cougar. He's in his office," Burke said, as he reached for the phone. He lifted the receiver. "Hello?"

"How are you, Delaney?"

Burke's hand clenched around the phone as he

heard the familiar high-pitched voice. "What do you want, Davis?"

"For you to suffer just like you made my sister suffer."

"I had nothing to do with your sister's problem, Davis, and you know it."

"That's what the judge and jury said, but you and I both know that you bought them off, don't we?"

"Look, Davis, you've been lucky so far. You haven't seriously hurt anyone. Stop it now before it goes any farther, and I won't press charges."

"Poor Miss Winston."

Burke's heart seemed to stop beating. "What?"

"Poor Miss Winston isn't feeling very well at the moment, but I'm afraid she's going to feel a whole lot worse very, very soon."

Burke closed his eyes and gritted his teeth against the nausea he could feel rising in his throat. "What have you done to Cara?"

"You were too well guarded, Mr. Delaney." The man gave a shrill laugh. "I couldn't get to you, but I got to her. My sister's left me, you know. So it's only fair that you lose someone you love too. Miss Winston's such a pretty thing, but she's going to pay for what you did to my sister. Then you're going to pay. Think about that for a while and suffer!"

The line went dead just as Cougar rushed into the room, carrying a small black box.

"Davis has Cara," Burke said dully.

"Did he say what he wants?" Cougar asked.

"He wants me."

"He didn't mention a ransom?"

Burke shook his head.

"What about some sort of deadline? Instructions of any sort?"

"Nothing." The numbness that had descended on Burke as soon as Davis had said he had Cara was beginning to recede, and in its place a cold rage was forming. He stood up and looked around. *"Dammit!"* With one sweep of his hand, papers went flying across the room. *"He's got Cara!"*

York and Rafe strode to his side immediately, flanking him.

"She's going to be all right," Rafe said. "Nothing is going to happen to her."

York placed his hand on Burke's shoulder. "He'll call again, and when he does, he'll give something away. We'll get him."

"York's right," Cougar said, placing a black box on the desk beside Burke's phone. "He's playing a game with you, and he'll definitely call again. When he does, we'll be ready." He opened the box and began hooking it to the phone. "This is the little gadget that's going to be his downfall."

"What is it?" Rafe asked.

"It's my latest toy. When Davis calls back, this will give us the number from which he's calling. Then it's a simple matter to get the address where that telephone is located. No need to say that it's not available at your local electronics store. Very few people have them."

"How did you get hold of one?" York asked.

"You can get anything you want if you have enough money and know the right people. I put my order in for one as soon as Davis stopped sending his charming notes. I guessed he might try to contact Burke by phone, but I'm afraid it never occurred to me that he'd go after Cara." He com-

pleted the hook up and turned to Burke. "I'm sorry,
Burke."

"It's not your fault. It's mine. I never should have
let her go out alone." He rubbed the back of his
neck. "I don't know what I'll do if anything hap-
pens to her. She's come to be my life." He swung
around to his brothers. "What can I do? I feel so
damn helpless!"

Rafe and York looked at Cougar.

"For the moment there's nothing we can do," he
answered. "We wait, I'm afraid. In the meantime
I'm going to check in with my men and find out if
they've seen anything downstairs."

Burke sat back down. With his elbows on the
desk and his hands folded, he stared at the phone,
willing it to ring.

*Don't be scared, Cara. I love you. I couldn't bear
it if I thought you were frightened or hurting.
Please don't be scared. Just hang on. Have faith
in me. I'll save you.* He repeated the same sen-
tences over and over in his head, as though if he
said them often enough, Cara would hear him.

Cara gradually awakened to the realization that
she couldn't move. Her head hurt, and her throat
felt dry. She attempted to swallow, but something
was in her mouth. She tried to bring a hand to her
face and found her hands bound to her sides. Then
she remembered.

The man who had come for her at the toy store
had been Davis. With a maniacal laugh he had told
her who he was right before he thrust the chloro-
form-soaked rag over her face. He had told her that

and something else that she couldn't seem to remember.

What a fool she had been to go with him, she thought, silently berating herself. Yet he had said something had happened to Burke, and she had seen the identification card. Her brain seemed to be operating sluggishly, but she forced herself to think. He must have taken it off one of Cougar's guards, and if he had disabled one of the guards, how many more could he have gotten to? Even now Burke could be in serious danger. The thought made her struggle desperately, but she had no coordination, and besides, her hands were held securely against her body by some sort of cloth rope.

Where was she? She could feel her muscles cramping at the unnatural positions they were being asked to hold. She was crammed half-standing in a very tight, dark space. She tried to straighten, but hit her head and heard a metal thud. She made an attempt to shift her weight, and her side hit a wall and created a sort of metallic clank. It was almost like she was in a tall metal cabinet of some sort. But it was so narrow! Could she possibly be in some sort of locker? And where?

And then she heard it—a faint ticking sound, directly above her. Something came back to her. The last word she had heard Davis say before blackness had claimed her. *Bomb.* Through the rag that he had stuffed in her mouth, she began to scream.

Time dragged. It had been fifteen minutes since Davis's call. Burke had taken off his jacket and tie, opened the buttons at his collar, and rolled up his shirt sleeves. His brothers had done the same. He glanced across the room at them, thankful that they were here with him. Their presence gave him comfort. They were talking quietly to one another. Their faces were grim, but if they were anything less than optimistic, he knew they would never let him know. They had spent much of the last fifteen minutes reassuring him.

Burke closed his eyes and began once again repeating his prayer to Cara. *I love you. . . . Please don't be scared. Just hang on. Have faith in me. I'll save you.*

Burke heard Cougar slam the receiver down on the phone, and he opened his eyes.

"One of my men has just been discovered unconscious, gagged, and tied up. The security of this building has been breached."

"That means Davis could be in the building somewhere," Rafe said.

"And so could Cara," York added.

"Cougar, how many men do you have on duty?" Before Cougar could answer, the phone rang, and Burke lunged for it. "I hope this is him. Hello, Davis?"

"You were expecting me. How nice."

In his peripheral vision, he saw Cougar, York, and Rafe cross to him. "Where have you got Cara?"

"She's gonna die soon now." Davis's laughter was earsplitting. "I hope the thought has given you half as much grief as I've had to bear. But you're not gonna have to suffer too much longer, because you'll be dead too. And guess what? I'm gonna watch the whole thing."

A number popped up on the screen of Cougar's

black box. Cougar looked at it, then ran to another phone and placed a call.

Burke covered the mouthpiece of the phone. "She's got to be here somewhere in this building. He says she and I are both going to die and he's going to watch."

"A bomb!" York whispered.

"Have you planted a bomb in this building, you bastard?" Burke yelled. "Is that what you've done?"

The line went dead amid shrieks of laughter. Burke pushed back his chair. "Cougar, we'll need the bomb squad. Call the police, then get you and your men out of the building, along with anyone else you find. I don't want to be responsible for needless deaths. Fortunately this is Saturday afternoon. There shouldn't be that many people here."

"I'm staying," Cougar said. "Davis is watching from across the street. I'll start searching immediately. The problem is, it's going to take a hell of a long time to search twenty floors. Maybe too long. Did Davis give you any indication where he put Cara?"

"No, but I'm going to get him now," Burke said grimly, already halfway out the door. "He'll either tell me or—" He stopped and threw a twisted smile over his shoulder at Cougar. "Try to find Cara before I kill him."

"Cougar's information is that the phone he used is in one of the ground-floor offices in the building across the street," Rafe said, "and I'm going with you."

"So am I," York said. "You'll need help searching those offices."

Burke didn't waste his breath arguing with them. He knew it wouldn't be any use.

Burke's hand quietly grasped the doorknob of the office door and turned. This was the third office he had searched. The other two had been empty. When they entered the building, he, York, and Rafe had split up. York and Rafe obviously hadn't had any better luck, or he would have heard something by now.

He pushed the door open and went in, being careful to tread softly. The room he had entered was a small reception area. His eyes quickly scanned the room as he moved through it. One more door. Cautiously he twisted the knob, then pushed the door slowly open. Disappointment shot through him as he realized this office was going to come up empty too.

He sensed the movement before he saw or felt anything, and that split second's warning saved him as he jerked his head to the side and spun at the same time. The butt of a gun whizzed by his temple. He grabbed Davis's arm and twisted, and Davis gave out a wild scream as the gun dropped from his grasp.

Burke continued to twist the man's arm high up behind his back, then shoved him hard against the wall. "Where is she, Davis? Tell me now and save yourself a lot of pain."

"No way, man," Davis said, panting. "Maybe you won't be in that building when it goes, but it won't be a total loss. This way I'll be able to see your face when we hear the explosion. I can't wait."

Burke let go of Davis's arm and jerked him

around. His dark green eyes had turned almost black with savage fury. "You'll tell me now or you'll die now! And you won't get to see or hear anything for the rest of your life."

"Then you had better hurry," Davis taunted. "The bomb may go off within the next few seconds. I've lost track of time and can't seem to remember when the bomb is set to explode. How about you? Do you know? It may go off at any moment, before you have a chance to kill me. And then the place where you knew such pleasure will become her tomb."

Davis's unnaturally shrill laughter was cut off by Burke's hands around his throat. The thought of Cara in danger, the thought of her in fear, the thought that he might never see her again, had driven him past the point of reason. His thumbs pressed into Davis's windpipe, and his hands began to squeeze tighter and tighter.

Burke felt hands on his shoulders. He heard Rafe and York talking to him, but he didn't know what they were saying. The next thing he knew, he was across the room and York's arms were around him, restraining him. Davis was lying on the floor, and Rafe was kneeling beside him.

Burke shook his head, willing his mind to begin functioning again. "Is he dead?"

Rafe's fingers were lying lightly over the pulse point on Davis's neck. "No. He's just unconscious. Did he tell you anything?"

"No." Burke rubbed his hands across his eyes. "Wait a minute! *Yes!* Dammit, yes." He broke free of York's hold and headed out the door on a dead run. "The gym," he called over his shoulder. "She's in the Delaney Tower gym."

*　　*　　*

Firmly blocking the sound of the ominous ticking from her mind, Cara concentrated on Burke. He would find her, she told herself. She knew he would. He had to. Their love was not going to end now.

She had learned so much since she had known Burke. She had learned that to know love, you had to possess the courage to reach out, to take hold, and to not let go. She had to tell Burke all this and so much more. The thought that he might never know of her love for him was unbearable.

She formed a picture of him in her mind. *He would find her. He would find her.*

"Cara! Cara!"

She could hear Burke calling her and the sound of locker doors being slammed back against one another. She tried to let him know where she was, but the gag and the swollen, raw condition of her throat hampered her.

Oh, no! A new thought had just occurred to her. What if the bomb went off now? It would take Burke too. She tried to scream in order to warn him, to give him enough time to get out, but the pitiful noises she was making couldn't be heard over the metal crash of the locker doors.

"Cara!" The locker door swung open and Burke reached for her. His only thought was that he was never going to let her go.

He had seen her tear-stained face and the terror that showed in her eyes before he had grabbed her, and it made him wish that he had killed Davis while he had had the chance.

"A bomb." She tried to get the words out so that he could hear her. "A bomb."

He was walking rapidly toward the door. Men in uniforms were swarming in. She saw Rafe, then York. They were running ahead of them, opening doors, clearing the way. She closed her eyes and lay her head against Burke's shoulder. Everything was going to be all right.

It wasn't until they were down on the street and a safe distance away from the building that Burke set her feet gently on the ground.

He stripped away the gag from her mouth. "Are you all right?"

She nodded.

"Forgive me, darling. Forgive me for putting you in such danger."

"There's nothing to forgive." The words were rasped out. "I'm just so glad you weren't hurt.

He untied the belt from a terry-cloth robe that Davis had used around her arms.

"Get a doctor over here!" Burke yelled toward a group of people standing around an ambulance.

"No," she whispered. "I'm fine."

"Maybe you should see a doctor, Cara," Rafe said gently. "You've been through a terrible ordeal."

She shook her head, but no one was listening to her. A paramedic came over and began checking her out.

A few minutes later York came running up. "The police chief just told me that they've successfully dismantled the bomb. We got out of there in the nick of time. It would have exploded within a few minutes."

Held securely against Burke's chest, Cara shuddered. "I want to go home."

"Home?" Burke asked, a cold dread settling in the pit of his stomach. After all she had been through, he supposed it was only natural that she would want to go back to Paris. But dammit! He couldn't lose her now!

"Burke," she whispered, "take me home to Killara."

Ten

From the top of the keep Burke and Cara had an awe-inspiring view of the sunset. Splendid colors splashed across the sky, vying with each other in their intensity—magenta, crimson, gold, vermilion. The sky seemed to sense the joy of the hour and bathed the land with the shimmering hues of fire.

Burke felt the peace and the joy, but he kept a watchful eye on Cara. "Are you sure you feel well enough to be up here?"

"I'm fine," she assured him, and smiled. They had flown back to Killara hours ago. Burke had clucked around her like a mother hen, practically hand-spooning hot tea with honey and lemon into her until Cara's throat felt much better. And when she said she couldn't take one more sip of tea, he had scooped her into his arms and carried her to bed. There he had held her close against him until she had dropped off to sleep.

"I feel recharged after my nap. Did you sleep too?"

He shook his head. "I watched you."

Lightly touching his cheek, she smiled. "No wonder I felt so secure." A caressing breeze tossed a silver-blond curl across her face. She pushed it away. "Thank you for bringing me up here. I didn't want to miss this sunset."

"Why this one in particular?"

"Because it's going to be very special. I can tell."

He pulled her against him so that her back rested against his chest. "I still remember that sunset a month ago when I first saw you riding Shalimar across the range." His mouth was over the opening of her ear, and when he spoke, his breath tickled warmly. "I thought you were a fantasy. I was right."

"I'm no fantasy."

"You're wrong. You're my fantasy, and I almost lost you."

Her lips curved tenderly. "When I was in that locker, waiting for you to come and rescue me . . ."

He turned her around to face him, and the expression on his face was grim. "I don't want you to think about it, Cara. It's over, and Davis will never have the opportunity to harm you again."

"I know, and I don't mind talking about it. I'm not afraid anymore, of anything." She touched his face, reassuring him. "It's important to me that I tell you what I was thinking during that time."

He looked at her doubtfully, but he was so glad to have her here with him, safe and smiling, that he would have granted her anything. "If you're sure, then."

"I'm sure. It's about you."

"Me?"

"When I was in that locker, the thought of you and all you've taught me sustained me. You've made me a better person, Burke. Being with you over this past month, I've gradually learned that love is worth all the risks. But I'm convinced that loving you has no risks."

His pulse began to beat faster. "What are you saying, Cara?"

She looked at him with unwavering gray eyes. "I'm saying that I love you."

He could hardly believe what he was hearing. "Is it really true?"

"I woke up this morning, saw you sleeping beside me, and all of a sudden I knew that I loved you. I'm only sorry it took me so long to figure it out."

His voice shook as he murmured, "Dear Lord in heaven, I love you so much." Slowly he pulled her to him and then his mouth lowered to hers with a kiss that held a deep and abiding tenderness and a promise of all that was to come.

"I love you too," she whispered when the kiss was over.

"I've wanted your love so desperately; I always believed you would grow to love me." Burke threw back his head and laughed with pure exultation. "You realize that I wouldn't have allowed anything else to happen, don't you?"

She grinned. "Oh, sure, now that it's all over, you can gloat, right? You're a formidable man, Burke Delaney, and I'll love you for the rest of my life."

"You'll never be able to tell me that often enough. Wait a minute! I just thought of something! We're going to be able to share our happiness with Rafe and York."

"How?"

"I was notified shortly before we came up here that York's helicopter landed on Killara out in the foothills, then took off again. The word is, he's not alone."

"What's he doing out there?"

"I don't know, but I'm sure we'll find out soon. And that's not all. Rafe radioed that his copter will be landing shortly. He's also bringing a guest."

"This is wonderful! We'll have a celebration."

"I bet we won't be the only couple celebrating either. I have a feeling that the future is going to hold only the very best for the Delaneys."

"I think you're right." Cara leaned her head against Burke's shoulder and thought of Killara.

Her life had come full circle. It had started on Killara and it would end here too. Killara's future would be her future. There would be children—hers and Burke's, perhaps Rafe's and York's too—to grow up strong and free. There would be much laughter and maybe a few tears. But always there would be love.

Looking toward the sun, she saw that the great fiery ball had almost disappeared. Now, though, she knew it would be back tomorrow. Secure in the knowledge of Burke's love, she was convinced that her moments in the sun were going to last for a lifetime.

THE EDITOR'S CORNER

Home for the Holidays! Certainly home is the nicest place to be in this upcoming season . . . and coming home, finding a home, perfecting one are key elements in each of our LOVESWEPTs next month.

First, in Peggy Webb's delightful **SCAMP OF SALTILLO,** LOVESWEPT #170, the heroine is setting up a new home in a small Mississippi town. Kate Midland is a witty, lovely, committed woman whose determination to save a magnolia tree imperiled by a construction crew brings her into face-to-face confrontation with Saltillo's mayor, Ben Adams. What a confrontation! What a mayor! Ben is self-confident, sensual, funny, generous . . . and perfect for Kate. But it takes a wacky mayoral race—including goats, bicycles, and kisses behind the bandstand—to bring these two fabulous people together. A romance with real heart and humor!

It is their homes—adjacent apartments—that bring together the heroine and hero in **FINNEGAN'S HIDEAWAY,** LOVESWEPT #171, by talented Sara Orwig. Lucy Reardon isn't really accident prone, but try to convince Finn Mundy of that. From the moment he spots the delectable-looking Lucy, her long, long shapely legs in black net stockings, he is falling . . . for her, with her, even

(continued)

off a ladder on top of her! But what are a few bruises, a minor broken arm compared to the enchantment and understanding Lucy offers? When Finn's brothers—and even his mother—show up on the doorstep, the scene is set for some even wilder misunderstandings and mishaps as Finn valiantly tries to handle that mob, his growing love for Lucy, law school exams, and his failing men's clothing business. A real charmer of a love story!

In the vivid, richly emotional **INHERITED,** LOVE-SWEPT #172, by gifted Marianne Shock, home is the source of a great deal of the conflict between heroine Tricia Riley and hero Chase Colby. Tricia's father hires Texas cowboy Chase to run Tricia's Virginia cattle ranch. Their attraction is instantaneous, explosive . . . as powerful as their apprehensions about sharing the running of the ranch. He brings her the gift of physical affection, for she was a child who lost her mother early in life and had never known her father's embrace or sweet words. She gives Chase the gift of emotional freedom and, at last, he can confide feelings he's never shared. But before these two ardent, needy people can come together both must deal with their troublesome pasts. A love story you'll cherish!

In **EMERALD FIRE,** LOVESWEPT #173, that marvelous storyteller Nancy Holder gives us a delightful couple in Stacy Livingston and Keith

(continued)

Mactavish . . . a man and a woman who seem worlds apart but couldn't be more alike at heart. And how does "home" play a part here? For both Stacy and Keith home means roots—his are in the exotic land of Hawaii, where ancestors and ancient gods are part of everyday life. Stacy has never felt she had any real roots, and has tried to find them in her work toward a degree as a marine biologist. Keith opens his arms and his home to her, sharing his large and loving family, his perceptions of sensual beauty and the real romance of life. You'll relish this exciting and provocative romance!

Home for the Holidays . . . in every heartwarming LOVESWEPT romance next month. Enjoy. And have a wonderful Thanksgiving celebration in your home!

Warm wishes,

Carolyn Nichols

Carolyn Nichols
  Editor
LOVESWEPT
Bantam Books, Inc.
666 Fifth Avenue
New York, NY 10103

His love for her is madness.
Her love for him is sin.

Sunshine
and
Shadow

by Sharon and Tom Curtis

COULD THEIR EXPLOSIVE LOVE BRIDGE THE CHASM BETWEEN TWO IMPOSSIBLY DIFFERENT WORLDS?

He thought there were no surprises left in the world ... but the sudden appearance of young Amish widow Susan Peachey was astonishing—and just the shock cynical Alan Wilde needed. She was a woman from another time, innocent, yet wise in ways he scarcely understood.

Irresistibly, Susan and Alan were drawn together to explore their wildly exotic differences. And soon they would discover something far greater—a rich emotional bond that transcended both of their worlds and linked them heart-to-heart ... until their need for each other became so overwhelming that there was no turning back. But would Susan have to sacrifice all she cherished for the uncertain joy of their forbidden love?

"Look for full details on how to win an authentic Amish quilt displaying the traditional 'Sunshine and Shadow' pattern in copies of SUNSHINE AND SHADOW or on displays at participating stores. No purchase necessary. Void where prohibited by law. Sweepstakes ends December 15, 1986."

Look for SUNSHINE AND SHADOW in your bookstore or use this coupon for ordering: